By Rachel Nickerson Luna
*Also from Emma Howard Books*

Darinka, the Little Artist Deer
Darinka's Nutcracker Ballet
Cape Cod Coloring Book
New York City's Central Park Color and Activity Book
Where Is Muffy Hiding?
The Thank You God Book

THE EEL GRASS GIRLS MYSTERIES

# Murder Aboard the California Girl

RACHEL NICKERSON LUNA

*Emma Howard Books*

NEW YORK CITY

# THE EEL GRASS GIRLS MYSTERIES
## Murder Aboard the California Girl
### By Rachel Nickerson Luna

© 2001 Rachel Nickerson Luna
Emma Howard Books, New York
Post Office Box 385, Planetarium Station
New York, New York 10024-0385

ISBN 1-886551-07-3
LOCCN: 2001087111

Manufactured in the United States of America

Cover Illustration Armando Luna

Kiki Black, Copy Editor
Book Design by Ian Luna
Typset in Mrs. Eaves Roman
Printing by Rolling Press
15-17 Denton Place, Brooklyn, New York 11215

Special thanks to
Moraiah Luna
Sophia Griscom

# Chapter One

Do you know what eel grass is? It's long, three feet long, thin grass that grows in patches in salt water. The eels hide in it, so it's creepy to step into it when you're launching your sailboat into the water. But it's everywhere along the shore. It can't be avoided. Just like us—the Eel Grass Girls.

We met last summer at the Yacht Harbor Sailing School. The Yacht Harbor Sailing Club is a cottage on top of a hill in a Cape Cod fishing village. The clubhouse overlooks Yacht Harbor, a stout harbor filled with fishing and pleasure boats of all shapes and sizes. The harbor opens up, past the old lighthouse, to the sea. It's always beautiful, whether sunny or overcast. Our summer life revolves around this harbor.

The four of us had decided to band together and form a mystery club. Nancy Drew and friends plus one. We were always looking for a mystery to solve. Who're the siblings of which classmates. Who left the peanut butter out in the club kitchen. Important things like that. Our motto is "Do the right thing." Not very original, but a good motto nonetheless.

Let me introduce the Girls. First there's me,

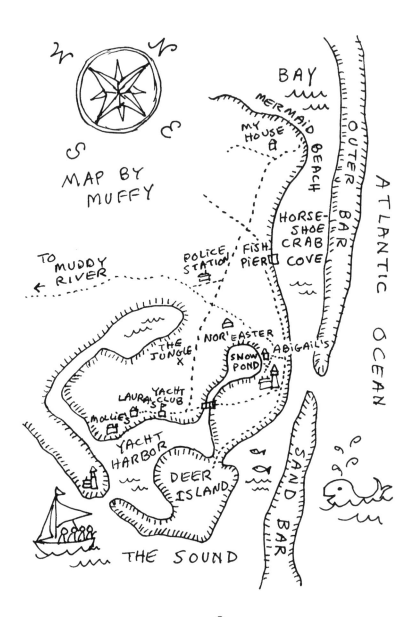

Muffy. My real name is Mora McLaughlin Cortez. It's a little different because my father is Filipino and my mother is an Irish–English blend. I'm proud of my name. I'm ten. I have brown hair and brown eyes. In fact, we all do. Only Mollie's hair is lighter than the rest of ours. It's almost blonde where the summer sun has bleached it. I live in New York City and come to Massachusetts for the summer. My mom grew up here so she wants me to have all the experiences she had growing up. So I'm obligated to sail, but it's fun! Abigail is from Connecticut. Her grandmother has a summer house here on Snow Pond. Her family stays there with the grammy. Laura has dark brown hair. She lives in town year-round. Her house is near the harbor. Mollie's family is from New Jersey. They have a huge summer house not far from the shore. Mollie is eleven, and Laura is nine and a half. Abigail is ten, like me.

None of us had ever sailed before. We didn't know a bow from a stern. Our instructors changed all that. We learned more last summer about sailing and Yacht Harbor than we wanted to learn. This is how it happened. The murder, I mean.

Abigail, Laura, Mollie, and I always stuck together at the club. We were the smallest girls, so we got to sail together when all the other boats carried only three sailors.

"Hey, bail out the bilge, Muffy!" yelled Mollie one Tuesday morning in mid-July. Why did she always make herself the skipper? Just because she was older didn't make her the boss!

"No can do!" I yelled back. "I'm getting the rudder and sails." As it was I had to make two trips to the bins where the equipment was kept to get everything we needed. With an instructor's help, we tilted the boat over to try to get the rainwater out of the bilge (the bottom of the boat), but it didn't work. Abigail, who never had an attitude, grabbed the old Clorox bottle, which was cut into a scoop, and pitched the water out onto the sand. Laura and I attached the sails and hoisted them up.

The other kids were doing the same thing to the other Sprites, the small fiberglass sailboats we used. They were lined up on the beach at the base of a cliff where wooden stairs led up to the Yacht Harbor Sailing Club.

The instructors, high school and college kids, helped us pull the boats down to the water. Then we got to push our boat out through the eel grass. It tickled our ankles and made us imagine that slimy eels were twisting around our lower extremities. We pushed until the boat floated, attached the rudder, jumped in, lowered the centerboard, and tried to sail between the piers into the harbor.

"Come about!" hollered Mollie as Laura steered our boat into a shellfishing dory moored near the town pier opposite the sailing club pier.

"It's O.K., Laura," I said. "Just tack over and we'll make it out of here." There really wasn't enough wind to tack because Deer Island, on the east side of the harbor, blocked the wind directly in front of the club. We had to force the bow of our boat around so it was pointed in the opposite direction. We drifted over to the club pier, then repeated the process, zigzagging by the town dock and out into the harbor. We continued toward Deer Island.

The water was murky green, filled with eel grass and all sorts of creatures: eels, minnows, crabs, and all kinds of fish. The light wind rippled the water, which lapped against the side of our little yellow boat, aptly named the *Minnow*.

Our classmates' boats were scattered around. The instructors in the club motor launches were trying to collect us all at the south end of the harbor, near a quiet beach, for a capsizing drill. It was a relatively open area with few moorings and little activity.

"Capsizing drill? Oh really?" laughed Mollie. "Those instructors just want to see us dripping wet."

"It'll be fun," added Abigail, the optimist. "At

least we'll know how to handle the worst thing that could happen to us, a capsize. We'll learn how to get the boat up when it goes over. Capsizing is the worst thing, right?"

"Uh-huh," I muttered as we approached a fishing boat moored near Deer Island. Lots of working boats were moored in the harbor among the pleasure boats, though most fishing boats were over in Horseshoe Crab Cove around the point. Actually it was an obstacle course getting around all the boats in this part of the harbor. We had to tack soon. We were headed in the opposite direction as the rest of the kids anyway.

Laura was still at the helm. "Come about! Come about!" ordered Mollie.

Laura panicked and pushed the tiller hard to leeward. Too late. We smacked into the fishing boat. I almost fell overboard.

"Wow, Laura!" exclaimed Mollie. "Let's inspect the damage."

"There's no damage, thank goodness," said Laura, looking over the edge of our Sprite. "I'm sorry! Is everyone all right?"

"We're all fine," I said as I stood up and peered into the fishing boat. That's when I saw it. The dead body.

"Ohmygod!" flew out of my mouth, even though I don't use that kind of language, and it's forbidden to swear on our boat. I don't like to throw God's name around, but it just came out.

"What's wrong? Is there a hole in the boat? Are we sinking?" called Abigail from the bow.

"We aren't sinking. I can see that there's no damage. What is it?" Mollie was pushing her way over to look.

I was silent as she moved over to the port side to stand beside me, looking into the *California Girl*, a beat-up old fishing boat about three times longer than our boat.

What met our eyes made us feel sick. I began to feel dizzy as if I would vomit. I turned away. Mollie kept on looking. For once she was speechless and couldn't think of anything to say. It was a man's body, lying face down on the deck. Blood flowed down from his head across the deck. The blood was bright red, fresh.

"What is it?" asked Abigail and Laura. We couldn't answer. Mollie and I moved away to let them have a look. They clambered up to the edge of the *California Girl*. They too were speechless.

"What is it?" they repeated again. They were so shocked they couldn't deal with what their eyes were seeing.

"It's a dead body," answered Mollie. "Wow, I think I'm going to puke." She was sitting down in the bilge holding her head, but she didn't throw up. We were all as pale as a fish's belly. Our eyes as big as quahog shells. Boy, were we shaken up and scared!

We all sat down and huddled together in the bilge. Our hearts were beating a mile a minute. We were in shock.

"What do we do now?" asked Laura.

"We're going to get the instructors—and quick," answered Mollie.

"Maybe he's not really dead. Maybe he's only hurt and we can help him," I said.

"I'm not going near him," said Mollie. "We'll wait here."

They weren't any help, but I didn't care. I was going to do the right thing. But it was as if I were in a dream. I hoisted myself over the side of the *California Girl* and moved toward the man. I felt his back. He was still warm. I tried to turn him over, but he was too heavy. I tried to find a pulse in his neck, but I didn't know exactly where to press my finger. I tried his wrist but found nothing. Either I was doing it wrong or I was just too scared. I went around to the other side to see his face. His blank staring eyes told the awful truth. I fainted.

# Chapter Two

"Wake up Muffy! Let's get out of here!" It was Mollie. She was beside me. Abigail had handed her a bailer full of harbor water. Mollie had dumped it over my head. I was fully conscious after that. We jumped back into the *Minnow* and pushed off in the direction of the instructors and the other kids. We sailed as fast as we could, but it seemed to take forever. We were yelling and waving our arms, but our voices were swept away by the slight wind that had come up as we got beyond Deer Island. No one noticed our frantic terror.

"I saw a dead body once," I offered as we crossed the channel and headed toward the instructors and the *Sea Calf*, the smaller of the club's two motor launches. "It was my dad's old boss. We went to the funeral home. He was there in a box. I didn't know he was going to be showing like that. I saw him before I could turn away. He looked gray. Like his spirit had left, and only a shell was there."

"I never saw a dead body," the others said. "But once my dog died," said Mollie. "He looked normal, as if he were sleeping, but stiff."

"My goldfish died," added Laura. "She didn't look asleep or normal. She was floating sideways with her eyes open."

"Stop!" screamed Abigail. "You're only making it worse. You act as if you don't care about that person we just saw."

"We do care," Mollie corrected. "We're just feeling weird and scared and trying to feel better by talking about it."

"But you're talking about an old gray man and your pets. This is a real person," complained Abigail.

Before we could argue any more about old men and pets being real people, we were close enough to the *Sea Calf* to get the instructors' attention.

"Doug! Jon! Something terrible has happened!" we screamed.

"What? You ran aground over at the Island?" asked Doug with a laugh.

"No! This is serious. There's a dead body in the fishing boat over there. Really!" insisted Mollie.

"Wow. Was it a flounder or a mackerel?" asked Jon.

"We're serious!" We were now right beside the *Sea Calf* so Laura climbed aboard. The rest of us followed. I tied the painter of the *Minnow* to the stern of the *Sea Calf*. When the instructors saw our faces, they knew  something was wrong.

"You say that there was a body?" asked Doug.

"A dead  body," corrected Mollie.

"Let's go check it out," said Jon.

"Shouldn't we tell Mr. Prince?" I asked. Mr. Prince was the sailing master, a husky middle-aged man, seemingly gruff, but really very caring. He was in the club's larger motor launch, the *Sea Cow*.

"Sure," agreed Doug.

"We've got trouble over here, Mr. Prince," he yelled, waving in the direction of Deer Island. Mr. Prince gave us an annoyed look. He had his hands full with all the boats overturned in the harbor. There were enough instructors in the water helping the kids so the little fleet was under control. But our emotions were way out of control as the *Sea Calf* sped toward the *California Girl*.

When we got to the fishing boat, the instructors pulled up alongside and peered over the edge.

"Where's the body?" asked Doug.

"Right on the deck," I answered as I peered over also. To my shock, the deck was clean! No body. No blood. The usual remains of fish guts and scum were clinging to the deck, but it had been washed down with salt water as after a fishing trip.

"Where *was* the body?" asked Jon.

"Right there." I pointed to the place. Nothing remained. Not even a trace of blood. "Someone washed the deck. Look below. They must have dragged him down below."

"Who dragged him?" questioned Jon.

"The murderers, of course," Mollie answered.

"I'm not going down there!" exclaimed Jon, "I'll radio the harbor master and let her take care of this." He tried to radio the harbor master, but she was busy with a fishing boat that had run aground on the other side of Deer Island, near Horseshoe Crab Cove. The Coast Guard was assisting her. So there was no one to investigate a dead body. How unfair, I thought. No one cares about this person, whoever he is.

# Chapter Three

The *Sea Calf* headed back toward the club. We were too shaken to do a capsizing drill now. We weren't even sure that Doug and Jon believed us.

"Don't worry, kids," said Doug, trying to comfort us. "The body is gone now."

"Yeah, right!" exclaimed Mollie. "No body so no big deal! They probably wrapped an anchor line around it and threw it overboard. I bet it's right down there in the water or it's still on the boat. Just because we can't see it at this moment doesn't mean it doesn't exist!"

"Save your breath, Mollie," I whispered. "He doesn't believe us. Maybe the police or the Coast Guard will."

"I'll take you kids to shore. Why don't you call your parents, if you're upset," Jon offered. He was trying to be nice, I suppose. He pulled the *Sea Calf* up to the yacht club dock. We untied the *Minnow* and sailed it the rest of the way to shore. We stood in the eel grass as we disengaged the rudder, pulled up the centerboard, and lowered the sails. We beached the boat and put the sails and rudder back in the bins.

All the other kids had turned their boats over in the shallow waters at the south end of the harbor and were struggling to get them upright again. We were missing all the fun, but we really were upset. We had to be brave, though. We were the only ones who had seen the body. The Eel Grass Girls had work to do. Neither our own fear nor two goofy teenage boys was going to stop us!

We strode up to the clubhouse and sat on the wooden benches lining the deck which overlooked the harbor. The warm breeze whipped the flagpole halyard and the yacht club flag, a gray seagull on a blue field. The real seagulls called and laughed overhead. The blue sky, filled with fluffy white clouds, was peaceful, oblivious to the murder that had been committed right beneath it. It was up to us, the Eel Grass Girls, to find the murderer.

"We'll go to the harbor master and find out who owns that boat," said Mollie.

"How do you know that she knows?" I asked.

"She does," Mollie stated. Mollie is such a know-it-all!

"Then we can go to the fish pier and ask around," suggested Laura.

Mollie countered, "Do you think those fishermen will tell us anything? We're just little kids. They won't tell us, especially if it's something bad about one of their own."

"You're always so negative, Mollie. Can't you ever be positive or hopeful, even just once?" I asked.

"I'm just being realistic. This isn't Hollywood. We can't write our own script," she responded.

"What are you talking about?" asked Abigail.

"Oh, never mind," said Mollie. "Here come the other kids."

We ran down the stairs to the beach. Jon and Doug, at Mr. Prince's orders, hadn't told any of the kids about the dead body. We were thankful, because we could proceed without a lot of dumb questions. The kids and the other instructors helped us pull the boats up to the tide line, which was marked by heaps of dead eel grass, dry and gray-black, filled with tiny seashells, sand fleas, and debris. We took down the sails, rinsed them, and spread them on the pier to dry. After we put the rudders away, we all ran up the stairs to the deck for our closing meeting. The sailing master discussed what the kids had done right and wrong during the capsizing drill.

The Eel Grass Girls were impatient to get out of there. We were reminded to bring a bag lunch to the next class for the Surprise Picnic, whatever that was. As soon as we were dismissed, Mr. Prince motioned to us that he wanted to talk to us alone. He asked us exactly what had happened and told us to tell our parents and have them call him if they wanted. That was nice of him. It was awkward, though, because it seemed that no one really believed us. We ran to our bikes and rode to Lowndes River where the bridge was.

# Chapter Four

The river connected the harbor to Snow Pond where the boatyard was and lots more moorings. There was a snack bar there called the Clam Bar, as in "sand bar." We could get hot dogs, chips, soda, and ice cream there. We needed to eat before we could think.

We got our lunch and sat on the riverbank to watch the water traffic and discuss what we would do next. We talked about what to tell our parents. We decided to tell about the body, but not our plan to solve the murder mystery. Tomorrow we would meet at the bandstand for lunch, but what should we do now?

"Let's ride to the lighthouse and talk to the Coast Guard," I suggested.

"No," protested Mollie. "We should call the harbor master first."

"Then let's split up. Muffy, you and I will go to the Coast Guard. Laura and Mollie will go to the fish pier to find the harbor master," suggested Abigail.

"Maybe no one is back from the wreck," said Laura.

"Well, there must be at least some 'coasties' still left on duty," stated Mollie.

We finished eating and rode our bikes over the wooden drawbridge spanning Lowndes River and on up the street to the lighthouse. Huge privet hedges and silver leaf trees shaded the road, hiding the sprawling lawns and rambling old homes from view.

Abigail and I stopped at the lighthouse as Laura and Mollie rode on toward the fish pier. We walked our bikes through the front gate and up a pathway of cement slabs to the Coast Guard station, just beside the light-house. The tower, used for weather warning flags and lights, stood tall on the lawn, overlooking the beach and bay, beyond which stretched the Atlantic Ocean.

Cautiously we entered through the broad red door. Inside the front hall we could see a petty officer on duty in the control room to the left. He asked us if he could help us.

"This morning while we were sailing in Yacht Harbor we saw the dead body of a man in a moored fishing boat called the *California Girl*," I blurted out all in one breath.

"A dead body, you say?" he repeated.

"Yes," we said in unison.

He looked at us, wondering, I guess, whether we were telling the truth or just playing a prank. He seemed to be considering why we would make the effort to come to him when we could cause as much mischief by just dialing 911.

"Have the police been notified?" he asked.

"No. Our sailing instructors radioed the harbor master, but she was helping with the wreck on the bar. She doesn't know about it yet," Abigail explained.

"O.K. girls. I have some extra men here who could go with you to check it out," he replied.

"The problem is," I put in, "the body disappeared."

"So," he began, rubbing his chin, "the body disappeared."

"Yes," I said. "We saw the body when our sailboat crashed into the *California Girl*. We got our instructors to come over in the launch to see it, but by the time we all got back there, the body was gone, and the blood was all washed away."

"Yeah," Abigail added. "Maybe someone was down below and heard us come on board. Then he, or they, whoever, may have stowed the body below or thrown it overboard with a weight tied to it. Then they must have washed down the deck because when we got back there with the instructors, there was no blood."

"Hmmmm. No blood," the officer repeated as he massaged his chin. "Hey, Pete! Joe!" he called.

25

Pete and Joe appeared. Young coasties in uniform.

"We have a launch at the town pier in Yacht Harbor as you know," the petty officer told us. To Pete and Joe, he added, "Take these girls down to the harbor in one of the trucks and check out the *California Girl* for a dead body. The girls will show you where it's moored."

Pete and Joe's eyes were popping out of their heads. "A *what*?" they asked.

"You heard me," the petty officer said. "See what you can find."

Abigail, the coasties, and I exited through the rear of the old station and drove down to the town pier. The orange and white launch, which looked like a heavy-duty inflatable kiddie pool, took us to the *California Girl*. Pete and Joe boarded and looked around the deck. Taking out a pad of paper, Pete jotted down documentation numbers from the side of the pilothouse. He and Joe went below. After a short while they were back.

"I found a few violations," he said, "but no body. The police might have a missing person's report in a few days. Then we'll maybe know who the guy was. With the documentation numbers we'll be able to check our computer and find out who the owner is. But without a body, there's not much we can do."

Abigail and I felt discouraged. Did anyone believe us?

26

"Did you look really well?" I asked. I was convinced that he hadn't done a thorough job. "I mean, did you check all the hatches, cupboards, and the engine room?"

"I looked around and didn't find anything," Joe said defensively.

"Well, we just wanted to make sure we weren't wasting our time here," I said.

"It's no waste. I found some violations, but that's all we have," was Pete's quick answer.

Oh boy! I thought. He doesn't believe us. Otherwise he wouldn't care about those violations, whatever they were. How frustrating! No one cares about the dead man! Then and there I made a plan. I would follow through, even if I had to do it alone. I felt desperate, but tried to calm down. My plan was crazy so I forced my brain to formulate "Plan B."

Abigail was looking at me with questioning eyes. "We have to go for Plan B," I told her in a whisper as we went the short distance from the *California Girl* to the town pier.

"What was Plan A?" she asked.

"I hope I never have to tell you," I said cryptically.

We thanked Pete and Joe for their time and trouble.

"No trouble," replied Pete as we piled back into the truck and headed for the lighthouse.

We all entered the station and listened to Pete and Joe tell the petty officer that they'd found no body, just a few violations. They checked the computer and found out the owner was a Dave Smythe from a town outside of Boston. He had no history of violations or trouble, but his name at least was something for us to continue our investigation. We thanked them and left by the front door.

"So what's Plan B?" asked Abigail as we got our bikes.

"Plan B is to find out who the crew members of the *California Girl* are and if they are all accounted for. If one is missing, he's probably the dead man."

"Maybe he wasn't even a crew member, but another fisherman who was fishing in their favorite spot or something," suggested Abigail.

"Could be, but he was on the boat. It seemed that the murder must have taken place there because of the fresh blood. You would think that someone over on the pier would have seen or heard something. They must have fought and argued. It must have happened while we were having our morning meeting up at the yacht club!" I added with a shudder.

"That fishing boat is behind those two big sailboats, and there are a few other good-sized boats between it and Deer Island," reasoned Abigail. "It's possible that no one saw or noticed. Even if the body was thrown overboard, it could have been done in an instant. No one would even notice the splash."

"But what happened to the murderer? How did he get away?" I asked her. "We didn't notice if a dingy was tied up to the boat when we crashed into it. How could he have had time to hide the body, wash the deck, and then get away all while we sailed over to the instructors and came back in the launch? It couldn't have taken more than 15 or 20 minutes."

"Murderers work fast when they don't want to get caught," Abigail answered. "He could have hidden on another boat or even been in the water and then swum to shore, but we've got to find out who he is. So what's next?"

"O.K.," I said slowly. "Next we have to think of every fisherman we know and ask them about this Dave Smythe and his crew, not that we know anything about commercial fishing. I guess it's time to find out. You go on home. I have to pass the fish pier on my way home, so I'll see what the other girls have found out. See you tomorrow at lunch. Remember, at the bandstand," I said. We rode in opposite directions. Abigail rode behind the lighthouse to her grandmother's house on Snow Pond, and I rode along the shore road to the pier.

# Chapter Five

Up and down the rolling hills I pedalled, past the big old houses facing the bay, to the fish pier. Mollie and Laura were no longer there, but the harbor master was. A weathered-looking woman about the age of my mom, she was talking to an agitated fisherman who was complaining. "If it wasn't for those d--- quotas, I wouldn't have to push myself to get over the bar in this tide, just to get myself an extra day of fishing. I can't afford to wait for the tide."

" Well, it's a miracle we got you off the bar. With all the Coast Guard cutbacks, half the time we don't even have the cutter here to help, but today you were lucky. We got you off, saved your boat, and you didn't lose your catch. You should be thankful and more careful next time," admonished the harbor master.

"I'd be more thankful if the U.S. government would let us make a living and give the Coast Guard the funding and manpower they need to do their job," declared the fisherman. He then turned abruptly and walked back to his boat, which was being unloaded at the pier. I saw my chance to talk to the harbor master.

"Excuse me, Ma'm?" I began.

"You don't have to call me 'Ma'm.' My name is Jan," she said. I knew that. Why wasn't she called the "harbor mistress" anyway?

"O.K., Miss Jan. . .ummm. . .I uh. . .I want to know about a fishing boat called the *California Girl*," I stammered.

"What is it you want to know?" she asked, not seeming too shocked by my question, but peering intently into my eyes.

"Who are the crew members? Do they all seem to get along?" Ooops. I didn't mean to say that, even though I wanted to know the answer.

"They seem to get along the same as any other crew. Let's see, the *California Girl*. They just started fishing here in the spring. Came down from Gloucester. Dave Smythe, Joe Sullivan, Alex Nickerson, Lou Vienta, and, uh, some other guy. Can't think of his name," said Jan.

I wish I had had a piece of paper. I didn't think I could remember all those names, but I would have to try. I'll have to get a pencil and notepad.

"Do they ever have anyone else go with them?" I cautiously asked.

"Sometimes fishing boats will take on a new member in the summer or just once in a while to try someone out, but not usually. I haven't noticed or heard of anyone new, but then I don't hear and see everything," she said.

"Why all the questions?"

"I'll be honest with you," I said, looking around to make sure no one was listening. Tourists were milling about, watching the boats being unloaded, oohing and ahhhing at the sharks (dogfish), the catch of choice nowadays. I moved a little closer to her and lowered my voice.

"This morning my friends and I accidentally ran into the *California Girl*, literally, and saw a dead body lying on the deck. When we returned with our sailing instructors, the body was gone and the deck washed clean. We went to the Coast Guard, because you were busy with the boat which ran aground. The two coasties who came to the boat with us couldn't find the body either. So what do you think?" I blurted out.

"What did the guy look like?" Jan seemed completely unmoved by anything I was saying.

"He had dark hair. He was big. His shirt was a red. Blue jeans. Rubber boots." It was all I could remember.

"Did you see his face?" asked Jan.

"His eyes stared at me."

"Was he shot?"

"There was blood coming from his head somehow." I started feeling sick just thinking about it. Remembering. I looked down. I wanted to cry. I wanted

32

to be home with my mom. I wanted to go.

"Hmmm. Maybe it was just an accident. A bad fall. It happens sometimes on a boat. Wet. Slippery. Heavy equipment. And it could be almost anyone, with that description," she said, almost indifferently.

I couldn't believe it. I wanted to scream!

"What are you going to do about it?" I blurted out. Uh oh. That wasn't very tactful, but I waited for her reply.

"There's no body, so there's not much to do," she said without emotion. "You've told me and the Coast Guard. That's enough. We'll take it from here. We'll keep our eyes and ears open. Probably was an accident. The guy probably just got up and walked away, so don't worry about it." The look on Jan's face told me not to waste my breath. That frustration again! She wasn't going to do anything. She didn't believe me. She didn't care. Or so I thought.

"Could you let me know if one of the crew members never shows up again?" I asked. What else could I say? Though I was still shaken by the memory of seeing the body, I was furious.

Jan seemed a little irritated. "Fishing is a hard profession. There are a lot of problems now with the fishing banks being overfished and the stocks being depleted. Of course it's not only the American fishermen who are doing the overfishing. Foreign vessels drag the bottom and snag every living creature. The government is trying to help, but the local fishermen need to make a living. I'm not saying the incident you mentioned has anything to do with this, but tensions have been high. People are upset. I think you had better stop asking questions and stay out of this." She made this last statement with a slight edge in her voice.

That was strange. First she says it's only an accident, then that the fishermen have problems and shouldn't be blamed for committing murder! Then she threatens me and tells me to "stay out of it." Very interesting. I'll definitely put this piece of information into my Eel Grass file.

"Thanks," I muttered. I turned my bike around and headed up the hill to the shore road. Was this mystery making more sense or less? On one hand I felt determined to solve this mystery with the help of the Eel Grass Girls, but on the other hand I felt powerless. I pedalled home. Home to safety. Home to sanctuary.

# Chapter Six

I got to our little cottage in the pines. It was cool and refreshing there. "Mom!" I called, bursting through the screen door. A piece of paper in the middle of the floor read, "Gone to Mermaid Beach with Sherry. Put on your swimsuit and come on down."

Great! I didn't feel like going anywhere. All this excitement had made me tired. I'll just read for a while, I thought. I entered my bedroom, plopped on the bed, and picked up the book I had been reading, *Nancy Drew*. No, no, no! Not *Nancy Drew*! Too much mystery for me. I was a failure as an Eel Grass Girl. We were supposed to be invincible, brave, and all that kind of stuff. I felt weak and frustrated. No bright ideas. All I wanted was my mom! I dutifully put on my new swimsuit, a colorful tie-dye with a matching wraparound skirt, went out to my trusty steed (my bike), and rode down to Mermaid Beach.

I spotted Mom and Sherry, her old friend from high school, who still lived in the neighborhood. They were walking along, talking, and picking up shells. And pieces of glass, if I know my mom. A few years ago a big storm blew a bunch of houses off the outer bar, and they ended up on the shore of Mermaid Beach. Only the houses were in little pieces. Lots of window glass was shattered all through the sand. Also, the beach people like to drink so all their beer, wine, and booze bottles are swept onto the shore and fill the sand with their brown, green, and clear slivers. Mom spends hours picking up every piece she can find and saying that she must be the only one who picks up the glass, how could there be so much, and on and on and on. I can't complain because she says she's doing it for me so I won't cut my feet.

I ran over to them. "Hi Mom. Hi Sherry." Sherry waved at me.

"Hi sweetie. How was sailing school?" asked Mom. From the look on my face, Sherry knew that I had something to tell Mom. She tactfully moved away to gather some shells further down the beach.

"Something awful happened," I mumbled as I hugged her around the waist. She hugged back, but immediately tensed up.

"What happened? Did someone try to hurt you?" She was always thinking something weird. She was always afraid for me for some reason, mother stuff I guess, but I thought she was overprotective.

"We found a dead body," I told her.

"Who found it? Where? Who was it? Did you tell the police?"

I told her the whole story, except that the harbor master had told me to essentially forget about it and that it was dangerous.

"Wow!" was all she could say for a while. "Well, I believe you, that there was a body. The Coast Guard and harbor master will find the murderer. Stay away from that boat. Don't go near it when you're sailing," she admonished. "I don't want you mixed up with any fisherman business. Do you understand?"

"Yes, I understand," I murmured. I understand that you don't want me to get in trouble, but I plan to find out who did it, I added to myself. I let her hold me and kiss the top of my head. I clung to her for a little longer. Then I let go and looked up into her face and smiled. I had the prettiest and best mother in the world. She would do just what I planned to do if she were still a kid. But now she was old and thought it was best to let "the authorities" handle the problem. Not because she really thought that they would do a good job, but because she didn't want me to get hurt. That's the way it is supposed to be. But I am a kid. I have to do what has to be done. The Eel Grass Girls must live by their credo: "Do the right thing." It's not original, as I've said, but it's true and it's good. Of course we should obey our parents, but there are times when what's right is different from what an adult tells you. Then it's a sticky situation, as you'll see...

# Chapter Seven

The next day, Wednesday to be exact, the Eel Grass Girls met for lunch in the park at the bandstand, a pretty white gazebo where the town band played to a huge crowd every Saturday night throughout the summer. A place full of wonderful memories, but so different now that it stood deserted in the bright daylight. We all had told our parents about what had happened, of course, and were still shaken about the dead man. Abigail had had a nightmare, but we decided that we were the Eel Grass Girls and we were going to solve this mystery.

Mollie and Laura told us that the harbor master had been out with the grounded fishing boat when they had arrived at the fish pier, and none of the other boats were unloading at that time either. They had considered questioning some of the workers who unloaded and packed the fish, but the work area was off-limits to non-employees. I told them about our excursion with the coasties to the *California Girl* and what the harbor master had said. We now had the names of the crew and some questions about a very strange harbor master.

"There's a fisherman who goes to our church,"

said Laura. "I could talk to him on Sunday."

"Let me step into my office and check my files," said Mollie. She looked under the tongue of her sneaker as if she were really reading something. We giggled whenever she did this. It really was funny. "Ah yes, my neighbor is also a fisherman. I can interrogate him tonight."

"How about just asking him a few friendly questions?" I asked.

"Such as, 'Do you know any murderers?' or 'Who on the *California Girl* would kill someone?'" Mollie joked.

"It's not funny," scolded Abigail.

"We know it's not funny," said Laura, "but I'm tired of being so serious, even if it is a murder."

"Let's go over to the Nor'easter Tavern and talk to some fishermen at the bar," I suggested.

"What?! Are you crazy? Kids aren't allowed in there!" exclaimed Mollie.

"I know, but we can go in on the restaurant side, sneak into the bar, and at least ask a waitress about the captain and crew. We know who owns the boat and the names of all the crew, but we don't know how any of them look. Maybe some of them will be in there and we can talk to them," I added.

"Sure," said Mollie, as sarcastically as possible.

"The part about the waitress makes sense.

Let's do that," suggested Abigail.

We walked across Main Street to the Nor'easter and entered the restaurant. It was busy with tourist families, summer people (those who owned second homes in town), and a few locals who had braved the crowds to get into town and find a place to eat. We slipped in to the back passageway leading to the kitchen, restrooms, and the bar. A frizzy-haired blonde waitress in cutoff jeans and a carpenter's apron passed by from the kitchen laden with burgers and fries.

"Excuse me, Miss," began Mollie, "We're looking for the crew of the *California Girl*. Are any of them in the bar?"

The waitress looked down at Mollie, then at each of us. She shrugged her shoulders.

"That's that new boat from off-Cape," she mused. "Alex Nickerson's on it. He's near the window up front. He has a beard, and I think he's wearing a blue plaid shirt. Some of the others are with him. What's up with you kids anyway?"

She eyed us suspiciously as we stared blankly back. Just at the last moment Mollie spoke up, "We're doing a school report on fishing, and we wanted to talk to some real fishermen about it."

"You kids aren't allowed in the bar. I'll ask Alex to meet you here, if he's in the mood. Isn't school out for the summer?" she questioned.

"Those mean teachers gave us a summer assignment," complained Mollie, in a very convincing way. I wondered if she lied this way to her mother.

The waitress continued into the bar. We followed to the doorway and peered around the corner. The floor, walls, and ceiling were made of dark, rough wood. The air was thick with smoke and the smell of beer. We gagged and blinked our smarting eyes.

"How can they stand it in here?" Abigail asked.

The waitress plunked the plates down on a table near the front window and spoke to a man we presumed to be Alex Nickerson. He looked over our way. We jerked back around the corner, then wondered why we were hiding.

In a moment Alex was standing before us, questioning with his eyes. "You want to know about fishing?" he asked in a soft, deep voice.

"Yes, about fishing boats in particular." Leave it to Mollie to have a ready answer.

Alex gave us a blank look. "What is it you want to know?" he asked, leaning against the wall. I wished that we could ask him what we really wanted to know. He seemed like a nice guy: big and gentle. Could he have become so angry that he killed a crew member? Could he be hiding a dark secret?

"We have to do a school report over the summer on a local industry and we chose fishing. We don't know anything so we thought that maybe you could show us your boat and tell us all about what you do," chattered Mollie.

"I don't see why not," he drawled. He paused, then asked, "How did I get to be the lucky one?"

"Excuse me?" Mollie didn't know what he meant.

"How did you chose me to be your guide?" he asked, smiling a little.

"Oh," Mollie was stuck. She looked at me in a panic. I had to think quickly.

"Because of your name," I spoke up. "The Nickersons are famous fishermen in this town, so you seemed to be the logical choice."

Alex smiled broadly now and seemed pleased with that answer. "My father and grandfather were fishermen, back to my great-grandfather." His eyes suddenly clouded over, and his whole demeanor changed as he added, "Things are different now. I have to work for that wash-ashore from Boston!"

"Pardon?" Laura didn't understand. Neither did the rest of us.

"Never mind," said Alex. He seemed more sad than angry now. "When do you want to see the boat?"

"Anytime you're free," said Mollie. She wanted to

close the deal as they say.

"How about after lunch? I'll meet you down at the town dock at Yacht Harbor at two o'clock. We'll row out in the dory and I'll show you around."

"Great!" The deal was made. "We'll see you there." It was better than we had hoped. We almost squealed with delight. Alex sauntered back to his table. I peered around the corner for a good-bye look at Alex just in time to see one of the other men angrily stand up, upsetting his chair, causing it to crash to the floor. He began to argue with Alex and shove him. Then the man stomped out the front door and disappeared. Alex and the others settled down again to eat.

"What happened?" asked Abigail as we went back through the restaurant and out onto the sidewalk to our bikes. We'd left them in the alleyway leaning against the side of the gray-shingled building.

"One of the other guys was arguing with Alex. Maybe he's the murderer and doesn't want us to go on the boat," I answered.

"You mean Alex?" asked Laura.

"No, silly, the other guy," said Mollie.

"What did he look like?" asked Laura.

Just then we heard the sound of a racing engine and gravel being torn up from the parking lot behind the

Nor'easter. We turned to see a red truck tearing out through the alley. We shrieked as we leapt around the corner onto the sidewalk in front of the restaurant just in time to avoid being run over. The truck plunged onto Main Street in front of cars coming in both directions, forcing them all to slam on their brakes to avoid hitting it.

"Wow!" exclaimed Abigail, "We almost got killed! Did you get the license plate number? Did you see who it was?" Traffic halted as everyone on and off the street stared after the truck as it headed off the Main Street toward the shore.

"It was him! The one who argued with Alex. I couldn't get the number. I was busy not getting killed!" I said.

"Well, he's obviously the murderer," said Mollie. "We have our proof. He argued with Alex, and he tried to kill us. It's time to go to the police."

"Wait a minute," said Abigail. "All of that is circumstantial evidence."

"What?" asked Laura.

"My father is a lawyer. He says that you need real proof, not just things that look like proof because you're suspecting someone. That fisherman may have been upset because his burger was overcooked. We may have just been in his way when he barreled out of here. He started accelerating before he saw us. He didn't know we were standing in the alley," said Abigail.

"You're so picky," complained Mollie.

We didn't quite know what to do next. We were still trembling from almost being hit by the truck.

"We have about two hours until our rendezvous at the dock so why don't we go to the Eel Grass Palace?" I suggested.

"Great idea!" the Girls exclaimed.

# Chapter Eight

Though we were still upset, we knew that a trip to our "palace" would make us feel better. The Eel Grass Palace was our secret hiding place or clubhouse. It was off Yacht Harbor Road, near the sailing club. There is a vacant field there, surrounded by an old split-rail fence, where a small sail loft once stood, A sail loft is where sails were dried in the olden days. Across the field, in back, out of sight to all passersby, is a tangle of wild grapevines which we call the "Jungle." The vines have grown up and over the old vines for so many years that the ones underneath have died and dried out, forming cavelike structures— almost like a village.

We each have our own house, as we call them. The floors are covered with dried eel grass. Each of us has decorated her house to suit her taste, with seashells, shiny rocks, and moss. Our clubroom is the largest house and contains our money box, an empty vanilla bottle for "aromatherapy," and some antique bottles and china we found in an old dump behind a nearby barn. One house, called "the tomb," contains the skeleton of a dead crow which we keep and look at each time we visit the Jungle.

There is an old dirt road which borders the field. We passed down it on our bikes, smelling the wild roses and admiring the shocking orange day lilies growing in a huge mass to our right. The road used to lead to a cranberry bog, but it has fallen into disuse and is now covered with bushes and cedar trees. We followed a path to the Jungle and went to our secret clubhouse to perform our ritual.

We have an old biscuit tin which I found in my grandmother's cellar. It contains a bag of marshmallows. Without a word, Mollie took a cardboard box of kitchen matches from our money box and lit a fire made of dried twigs surrounded by rocks. Each of us took a long stick from the ceiling of our clubhouse, pushed a marshmallow onto the end, and began to roast it. After we partook of our ritual meal and extinguished our fire, we looked in on the crow's skeleton. Then we went to our individual houses to straighten up.

"Hey, someone's been in my house!" yelled Laura.

We all crowded in to see. Her seaweed was messed up.

"Eeeeew! Coyote poop! That's disgusting!" We all observed the offending specimen.

"It's fox poop. There're grapes in it," I pointed out.

"Yuck! Whatever it is," groaned Laura, "I have to move."

"We'll help you," offered Abigail.

All of us gathered up the eel grass and the poop, carried it near the old bog, and threw it into a clump of birdberry bushes.

"Shall we gather some new eel grass now?" asked Abigail.

"Not now," said Mollie. "We'll get it after we go on the boat. Let's find a new house for Laura."

We searched the Jungle. Laura found a nice new house with green vines growing inside. I wondered how we could have missed this one. It looked more beautiful than any of ours. We gathered lots of twigs and brambles and filled up the old house to keep the fox out.

"Will that keep the fox from coming back?" asked Laura.

"Maybe if we pee in our houses that will keep him away," said Mollie.

"You are so gross!" hollered Laura. "Why should I do what I don't want the fox to do?"

"Pee and poop are two different things. I'm being scientific. It's what animals do to stake out their territory," Mollie said defensively.

"I hate to change the subject, but it's time to go," I said, looking at my watch.

We straightened up and went out to our bikes. As we rode onto Yacht Harbor Road toward the dock, we heard a noise behind us in the distance, getting louder. It was a vehicle traveling too fast. I turned to look over my shoulder and saw the red truck plowing down the road behind us, too close to the edge of the road.

"Watch out!" I screamed as I leapt off my bike, over the fence, and into the field. The others followed, leaving their bikes on the side of the road. The truck's wheels barely missed hitting the bikes. It sped off down the road toward the dock.

"Is everyone alright?" I asked as we looked ourselves and each other over to make sure that we were O.K.

"I'm a little bruised," said Laura.

"Me too," Abigail chimed in.

"Let's go get that smelly fisherman!" yelled Mollie. "He's not going to get away with this again. Guilty of murder or not, he's guilty of trying to kill us twice, whether you agree or not!"

She hopped on her bike and started pedalling toward the town dock. We followed. When we arrived we saw the red truck in the parking lot. Now I had a pad of paper in my pocket so I jotted down the license plate number. Mollie was right about one thing: he wasn't going to get away this time.

When we reached the dock, we saw a mean, scruffy-looking fisherman rowing hard out to the *California Girl*.

We hid ourselves behind a stack of wooden boxes on the pier and watched the boat. We could see Alex and some other men moving about on deck. We tried to count them to see if any were missing. We counted five. No one was missing. They were probably getting ready to go out, even though it didn't seem like the right time of day to go out on a fishing trip. But how would we know?

"Well, so much for our tour of the *California Girl*," said Laura.

"I'll get that fisherman sooner or later," muttered Mollie.

"I've got his license," I said. "We never told the police about the murder. Now I think we should. We know which of those men has a guilty conscience. We know what he looks like, but we need his name."

Abigail asked, "What do we do now?"

"How about ice cream at the Clam Bar?" suggested Laura. We all agreed on that and rode our bikes over. We ordered our favorite flavors and sat on the bank of Lowndes River to lick our cones. Mollie was still fuming about the fisherman in the red truck. We finished our ice cream and decided to go over to the shore and wait to see if the boat really went out.

We rode back past the town pier and the sailing club to the shore where we could comfortably watch the

*California Girl*. Some of the yacht club families had boat-houses there. Dinghies lined the beach. We looked for shells and poked around in the eel grass, all the while keeping an eye on the fishing boat. To our dismay, the fishermen were watching us too. The one who had almost run us over pointed at us and made a call on his cell phone. It was too late to hide. We had been careless. But they were on their boat. They couldn't hurt us from there. Besides, the fishermen seemed very tense. A few arguments sprang up as the crew prepared to leave port. Finally they cruised out of the harbor and on out to sea.

"They know that we know. I bet that scruffy-looking one is the murderer. Maybe he's Smythe," concluded Mollie.

"Let's try to find out which one is which. We know Alex Nickerson. Shall we ask the waitress at the Nor'easter?" asked Abigail.

"It might be safer for Laura to ask the fisherman at her church than for us to go back into that bar. Or Mollie, can you ask your neighbor? He could tell us. Maybe we could all interview him," I suggested.

"Why didn't I think of that?" Mollie asked herself. "I heard him come in late last night. He's probably puttering around fixing his lobsterpots by now. Let's go."

# Chapter Nine

We rode up the hill and onto the shaded road leading to Mollie's house. The scrub pines and oaks covered the land which, a hundred years ago, was farmland. Her long driveway was covered with white shells, gleaming in the bright summer sun. Off to the right was a dirt driveway leading to an old farmhouse and barn owned by Howard Snow, Mollie's fisherman neighbor. Lobsterpots and all sorts of driftwood and old crates were heaped in piles beside towers of smelly mussel shells. A burly man of about thirty was bustling around in front of the barn when we arrived.

"Hey, little neighbor!" he greeted Mollie.

"Hi Howard! These are my friends, the Eel...er...Laura, Abigail, and Muffy. They're the girls I told you about, from the yacht club," muttered Mollie. I couldn't believe that she almost gave away our secret name!

"Nice to meet ya." Howard gave us a big, easy grin. "What are you girls up to on such a nice day?" I guess it was obvious that we were "up to" something!

"Remember how I once told you that my friends

and I like to solve mysteries?" began Mollie. The three of us were shocked and gave her the most evil looks imaginable. How could she disclose our secret mission to anyone? Especially her neighbor. Who was a guy.

Mollie squirmed a little under our icy gazes, but went on, "We need some information about some fishermen." Why couldn't she just continue with the "school report over the summer" line?

"What kind a information?" asked Howard, seeming to me to become a little uncomfortable.

"Oh, about personalities on a certain fishing boat. That sort of thing," Mollie continued breezily.

"Who're ya interested in?" he asked.

"The *California Girl* crew," blurted out Mollie. I had a bad feeling about this interview, but there was no stopping her.

"Why?" asked Howard, now a little more tense and not so friendly anymore.

"It's part of our mystery," bubbled Mollie. "Can you tell us about the owner and crew? What they look like? What kind of trucks they drive? All that sort of thing."

Howard looked from one of us to the other. "Why don't you girls find another mystery to solve?"

"Why? The mystery already exists. What do you know?" asked Mollie.

"I don't know anything about your mystery, and I don't want to know. That's a bad boat. I've heard stuff. Stuff you'd better leave alone," he added sternly.

"What have you heard? It may be important. It might help us solve our mystery," pleaded Mollie.

"I ain't tellin' nothin.' Some things aren't meant to be repeated. They're just rumors. Some things you hear it's best to forget." He looked sullen now. "You'd better go on now and stay away from that boat and whatever your mystery is. Forget it!" With that, he turned his back on us, resumed his puttering, and ignored us.

# Chapter Ten

We stood in the driveway staring at each other. Mollie was the first to mount her bike. With a nod of her head, she motioned us to follow her down the driveway to her house. When we got there we went around to the back, which faced the harbor. The gentle breeze blew off the water over the bluff where we sat.

"Wow!" exclaimed Mollie. "Is he hiding something or what!"

"How could you tell him about our club?" I asked. "We promised never to tell anyone! You almost told him our secret name! Maybe you already did! You're a traitor!" I was really angry at her.

"I didn't tell. One day we were talking, and it just came out. We were telling each other about our friends and hobbies. I never thought you all would end up meeting him. I didn't think . . ."

"That's right. You didn't think. Next time don't tell anyone anything. This Howard person is probably a part of this murder and now he knows too much about *us*. You shouldn't have told him so much. You should have stuck to your school report story. Now we're really in trouble. We not only have the red truck guy after us, but now Howard might be after us too." I was beginning to sound like Mollie. It didn't make me feel good about myself.

"I thought we could trust Howard. I never thought he would become so weird. I thought we could get some good information from him. I don't think he'll hurt us though." She looked up at us with her big brown eyes. "Sorry!"

"Forgiven," we answered.

"I hope that fisherman at my church doesn't turn out the same way!" exclaimed Laura.

We all agreed. We had no idea what to do next. We needed more information about the fisherman in the red truck. He was the most aggressive. I voted for asking the waitress.

"What if she tells him?" inquired Laura.

"He's out fishing for a few days now, so she'll probably forget by the time he gets back," said Abigail.

"I'll stop by there on my way home. Then I'll go to the police," I suggested.

"Don't you want us to go with you to the police?" asked Laura.

"No. I'll report the truck. The waitress will probably be able to tell me who the owner is. Or the police will," I said.

"It's up to you," said Mollie.

We were quiet for a while. All this mystery stuff was taking the fun out of our summer. We needed a break so we decided to go for a swim. It was so hot. We changed into swimwear. Mollie had extra suits. Her last year's suits no longer fit her, but they fit me and Laura. She had a spare for Abigail, who was about her size. We then ran down the bluff to the beach.

After a refreshing swim, we dried off on Mollie's beach towels and then found some nice seaweed to take to Laura's new house in the Jungle. We visited the Jungle just to drop off the eel grass. No more fox activity! We made a plan to talk the next day at our sailing lesson. We split up and headed in different directions. I rode down to the Nor'easter. Laura went off to a tennis lesson. Mollie had to do some summer reading, and Abigail had a grammy obligation.

# Chapter Eleven

I entered on the restaurant side of the establishment and looked for the frizzy-haired blonde waitress again. She wasn't there. As I walked into the back hallway and peered into the bar, I heard, "Muffy!"

I nearly jumped as I spun around to see one of our instructors, Billy Jones, leaning out of the kitchen door. Why was I so jumpy?

"What are you doing here?" he asked. I wanted to ask him the same thing.

"I...uh...was...um...looking for that waitress with the blonde, frizzy hair."

"Oh, Linda. She's off today." Billy waited for me to say something. I knew he wouldn't fall for the "school report over the summer" story, but I didn't want to tell him the truth. Maybe he could help me, though.

"I need some information about some fishermen. I have almost all their names, but no descriptions to go with them. Do you know the *California Girl*?"

"That's the boat moored across from the club, where something happened yesterday, right?" he asked. "I heard from the guys that Mr. Prince told Jon and Doug not to talk about it. What happened anyway?"

"We saw a dead body lying on the deck, but no one believes us," I said.

"Wow! So that's what happened! The owner is a hot-headed guy from near Boston. Big guy with a red truck. Dave something. The crew is mostly local, from here and Muddy River. My brother hangs out drinking with those guys." Billy gave me descriptions of all the crew. He also knew the name of the one the harbor master couldn't remember: Larry Knowles. I had my notepad and wrote it all down. We knew that the owner of the boat was the one who ran us off the road. Now I was going to the police.

"What are you going to do with all this information?" Billy asked.

"Secret girl stuff," I answered, as perky as Mollie would. It seemed to work on Billy.

"Do you work here?" I asked, making conversation.

"Yeah. I need the money for college. See you at sailing school tomorrow!" said Billy as I left. Then he warned, "Don't do anything dumb."

I gave him a "look" and exited.

Back on my bike, I pedalled down Main Street. The traffic was crawling on the narrow street. Cars were badly parked, with bumpers sticking out, a few cars going the wrong way. I wondered why tourists forget how to park when they're on vacation. Maybe they think that we're so provincial here we don't have any laws or maybe because they paid so much for their vacation, they think they can break the laws we do have. Whatever it is, it's annoying. Pedestrians jaywalk all over the place. I watched out for car doors opening suddenly so I would stay alive. I made it to the police station, which overlooks the town ball field.

I strolled into the station and hoped someone friendly would be on duty. An unpleasant-looking female officer greeted me with a stony gaze.

"Hi," I began. "I want to report a truck that almost ran over me and my friends."

"Name?" she demanded.

"My name or his?" I asked, not enjoying this process.

"*Yours*" was the lively response.

"Mu...Mora McLaughlin Cortez," I replied. My real name is quite a mouthful, I admit, but my Irish, English, and Filipino heritage is a great combination! I'm proof of it!

"Location?"

"On Yacht Harbor Road, just before Lowndes River Street."

"What exactly occurred?"

I told her the story. Since no one died, and there were no adult witnesses, nothing was going to happen. She wrote up a report and that was that.

"Did anyone report a murder the other day?" I asked nonchalantly.

She rummaged through some papers on her desk.

"Down at the harbor? Yeah, but no body."

"Is anyone reported missing?" I queried.

"No." Another lively and informative response.

"Thanks. Bye." I exited, more determined than ever to solve this murder mystery.

# Chapter Twelve

At dinner my parents asked me how my day had been. I said, "It was fine," not wanting to go into detail about Howard's warning and the nasty police officer. Not to mention almost being run down twice by the infamous red truck. Mom reminded me of the Surprise Picnic at sailing class the next day. I read some comics before bed. *Nancy Drew* was going back to the library. The Eel Grass Girls had a real mystery to solve, and it was stranger than fiction. Comics were all I could cope with right now.

The next morning, which was Thursday, I gobbled down breakfast and got ready for sailing school. I packed my bag with lunch, a bottle of water, and sunblock. Then I donned my blue Yacht Harbor Sailing Club hat (embroidered with a gray and white seagull), my sunglasses, and lifejacket. I changed into my water shoes (we were required to wear "proper" footgear on the boats), said good-bye to my parents, and rode down to the club. I kept thinking of Plan A, which had been discarded on Day One but seemed more and more necessary as time went on. I wasn't sure how to carry it out or which of the Eel Grass Girls would be able to assist me. How could I even get out of the house at night? What was Plan A? I'll tell you later.

Now it was time to sail. I parked my bike near the blackberry bushes beside the club and found the Girls. The sailing class sat on the wooden benches above the harbor. Today we were going "outside"! That meant we would go out of the harbor to the sound, which was practically the ocean! Wow! We'd never done that before. Mr. Prince said that because it was such a calm day, we would go out and see where the larger boats raced. Then we'd come back in for a picnic on the harbor beach just inside the cut-through which connected the harbor and the sound.

We prepared the boats and brought them to the water's edge. We were sure to get the *Minnow* again. No one ever tried to use it. They always let us take our favorite.

"Look at that creepy guy!" exclaimed Laura. We followed her gaze to a dark-haired, greasy-looking man with a red face and green flannel shirt. He was leering at us from the corner of an old shack near the town pier. "He keeps staring at us!"

"Should we tell the instructors?" asked Abigail.

"There's no law against staring," said Mollie.

"Let's just make sure he's not around after class. We'll have to stay together. My mom keeps telling me to be careful. I think she's right," I said.

We were herded into our boats and out onto the water. In no time our little fleet was sailing toward the cut-through and out to the sound. It was another beautiful day. So balmy and perfect.

"Howard won't even say 'Hi!' to me anymore," said Mollie. "I saw him coming out of his driveway this morning. He just scowled at me, then looked away. We used to be so close."

We didn't answer. She had told him too much and now he was our enemy, it seemed, instead of an ally. We splashed water at the boys in the boat nearest to us. Our bailer, the old Clorox bottle, was very handy for that.

"Your boat is poison!" we yelled. "Get away from us."

"Ewwww! Girls! You're poison!" they screamed back, splashing us with their bailer. It was so much fun getting them wet! We were better sailors than those boys too.

Mr. Prince and some of the instructors were in the *Sea Cow* and *Sea Calf*. Other instructors were in the Sprites with the kids who were not comfortable sailing by themselves. The channel led to the cut and through it. Beyond were the shifting sandbars leading into the sound. We tacked through the narrow cut. Pleasure boats and fishing craft were going in and out at the same time. We all had to be very careful.

It was a little breezy out in the sound. We were instructed to sail around a certain nun buoy and then back through the cut to the beach just inside the harbor. As we rounded the buoy, a motorboat caught our attention. It was going awfully fast—and it was headed straight toward us.

"What the...?" exclaimed Mollie. The motorboat was not that far away, and it was holding its course. It quickly neared us.

"Mr. Prince! Somebody! Help!!!" we all cried out. We screamed at the top of our lungs and flailed our arms in the air. The other sailboats saw what was happening. Tacking away from us and the danger, they headed toward the club launches.

Mr. Prince also saw what was going on. He blew his air horn to alert the motorboat and shouted through his megaphone for the boat to head off. It kept on, straight toward us. Mr. Prince also headed toward us to block the motorboat, but the big *Sea Cow* wasn't as fast as the smaller motorboat.

"We're all going to die!" wailed Mollie.

"No we're not! Jump!" I screamed as I dove into the water and swam behind the nun buoy. The other three followed my example and leapt into the dark, deep water after me, just in time. The motorboat plowed into our Sprite, the *Minnow*, crushing its bow beyond repair, ripping the jib off as it flew by. It kept on going. The driver kept low, but we all saw him. The creepy guy who had been leering at us from the town pier!

Mr. Prince arrived too late to save our boat.

"Are you alright?" he asked. "Is anyone hurt?"

The instructors and Mr. Prince helped us scramble into the *Sea Cow*. Mr. Prince directed the *Sea Calf* to assist the other sailors who were also shaken by the accident. We were shivering from the shock of almost being killed and from the cold water. Though it was really warm, the balmy breeze made us colder.

All this trauma was beginning to be too much for me. First a dead body, then the truck, now an accident which almost killed the four of us. I was just about ready to give up on this stupid mystery, but we were in too deep. There was no turning back. We had to solve it, because it wasn't going to go away. Even if we did forget about it, those men wouldn't leave us alone. They might think that we knew more than we did and wouldn't stop until we had an "accident" which would stop us.

Abigail and Laura were whimpering. I couldn't blame them. It had been the scariest moment of my life! I was shaking, but I was too angry to cry.

"Are you O.K.?" I asked the girls. I could see

that Mollie was angry too, so angry she was about ready to explode.

"We're alright," I told Mr. Prince. Two of the female instructors were rubbing our backs and arms and giving us sweatshirts and sweaters to wear.

"Does anyone know who that man was? Or why he would try to hurt you?" asked Mr. Prince.

Before anyone could answer, Billy Jones said, "I saw that guy in the Nor'easter last night. He was drinking with Dave Smythe, who is one of those out-of-town fishermen."

At that moment a light went on in Billy's head and in mine. He looked at me and I at him. Sooooo, we both thought, Dave Smythe has put his greasy friend up to terrorizing the little detectives, has he? The Eel Grass Girls weren't going to take this! This meant war. Not only for the crew of the *California Girl*, who were already attacking us, but for the Eel Grass Girls, who were now ready to go into battle against them! Anyway, I hoped that the Eel Grass Girls were still interested in going to battle. We huddled together and shivered. It looked doubtful.

My eyes pleaded with Billy not to say any more. Mr. Prince was radioing the harbor master. I gathered from Mr. Prince's side of the conversation that the harbor master was just inside the harbor. Mr. Prince gave her a description of the man and boat which were nearing the cut-through at that moment. Maybe the harbor master could catch him.

The instructors were hauling the wreck of the *Minnow* out of the water to keep her from sinking.

"The harbor master is on her way. She's just inside the harbor. She'll be here soon, if she doesn't catch that man first. They'll surely pass each other near the cut. So none of you know him?" asked Mr. Prince.

I told him that I had seen the man lurking around the town pier just before we came out, and that he had been leering at us.

"You should have told someone. You should have told me, and maybe this wouldn't have happened," he admonished. "But if you don't know him, why would he want to hurt you?" We just shrugged.

"Some people!" he exclaimed, "That man probably had too many beers with his lunch!"

No one laughed at his lame joke. Billy took me aside to a corner of the stern.

"What's the 'secret girl stuff' going on with you and Dave Smythe?" asked Billy. He was serious.

"What?" I didn't know what he was talking about.

"When you were at the Nor'easter yesterday, you

told me you wanted to know about Dave..."

I cut him off. "Oh, *that*...um...it's secret stuff...and...uh...it does have to do with us girls, but it's not 'girl stuff,'" I quickly explained, a little embarrassed.

"Yeah," he replied. "Clear as mud. Why don't you tell me why Smythe's friend would want to kill you cute little girls?"

I considered. Could we trust Billy? We found out that Mollie couldn't trust her friend Howard. Would Billy be any different? Would it be too risky to take a chance? Why should we tell? Billy wasn't exactly an adult, in our minds anyway. He was in college, but he acted like a kid.

"I'll have to consult with my associates," I said as I moved over to the others, who were huddled together shivering. Laura and Abigail had stopped crying, and Mollie was silent and sullen.

"Are you guys O.K.?" No one answered. Laura and Abigail looked at me with pleading eyes, as if they were saying "We've had enough of this mystery!" Mollie's eyes said, "I'm angry, but scared. This is more than I expected from a summer caper."

I began, "Yesterday when I went to the Nor'easter, the waitress wasn't there so I asked Billy about the fisherman Smythe. Now, because he saw Smythe and Mr.

Greasy drinking together, he knows that there's a connection. He wants to know what's going on. Should I tell him?"

"I don't care," sighed Abigail. Laura nodded. Mollie shrugged.

I started to feel alone. The Eel Grass Girls were deserting me. I couldn't blame them. This was worse than we ever expected. Did I want to include Billy? If he told any adult what we were doing, the adults would put a stop to it, and the mystery would never be solved. But did I want to go on alone?

"Do you all want to quit?" I asked, feeling a little annoyed, even though I knew I shouldn't blame them. I didn't want to go on all alone. I had thought I could depend on them, but could I even trust Billy?

There was no answer, but it was answer enough.

"O.K. then. I'm telling Billy." But before I could, the harbor master arrived, tied up to the *Sea Cow*, and hopped aboard. Mr. Prince told the instructors to take the fleet to the beach inside the harbor for the Surprise Picnic. Then he gave the harbor master an account of the accident and a description of the man and boat. Incredibly, the harbor master said she hadn't seen the motorboat enter the harbor! Was she blind? Or was she also part of it?

Mr. Prince directed the harbor master's attention to us, the crew of the ill-fated *Minnow*. It was Jan, of course. When she saw me, she immediately recognized me.

"Well, if it isn't little Miss Nancy Drew!" I turned bright red, I'm sure, and gave her a shocked and angry look. I was a little hurt, too. What right did she have to talk to me that way, in front of all the instructors and Mr. Prince? Why did she have to mention our "case"?

"Didn't I tell you to forget about your little mystery?" she asked, peering at me in an evil way. She suddenly seemed very nasty. Everyone was staring at me.

"Do you think this incident is connected?" I asked as innocently as possible, looking her directly in the eye.

She seemed a little shocked. Of course there was no obvious connection, and there wouldn't be. Unless a person knew about the murder on Smythe's boat and the fact that the person who tried to sink us was Smythe's friend. Jan supposedly hadn't even seen the man or his boat. How was it that she could make any connection at all unless she knew more about it? Maybe even more than we did.

"Who was the man who rammed your boat?" she asked, changing the subject and not answering my question.

"We don't know," I answered, leaving it at that. I got the feeling that Mr. Prince and Billy were also suspicious of her.

Billy told Jan that the man in the boat was at the Nor'easter last night talking with Dave Smythe. Everyone agreed that he wasn't a local. Jan seemed to be thinking. If we all knew that the man was talking with Smythe and then he tried to kill us, now we all knew there was probably some kind of connection.

"You girls alright?" she asked, changing the subject again.

We nodded weakly. Jan suddenly seemed anxious to wrap up her investigation and leave.

"You didn't see that motorboat enter the harbor?" Mr. Prince asked again. The boat couldn't have gotten past the harbor master and just disappeared!

"There were a lot of guys fishing in the channel, and I was hurrying to get out here," was Jan's weak excuse. She turned, boarded her boat, and left. Mr. Prince rolled his eyes behind Jan's back. As soon as the harbor master's launch had left, Mr. Prince said, "Maybe Jan is that man's cousin. She must have seen that guy. I'm calling the police."

He radioed the police who informed him that the harbor master would take care of it. She was capable of handling the investigation. Great! I wondered if Officer Personality was the officer on duty.

This had been the most interesting week at sailing

school I had ever had. I was glad that classes were now only two days a week. I didn't think I could stand another day of this. Not this week anyway. I couldn't think of racing. I was beginning to have a fear of boats!

We followed the fleet to the beach. We didn't want to picnic. I saw Billy talking to Mr. Prince, who turned to us.

"Billy will take you girls back to the club in the *Sea Calf*, and you can call your parents to come pick you up. I'm really sorry about this. Your parents can call me." Mr. Prince was so nice. He was probably afraid that our parents would somehow blame at him for what had happened, but it wasn't his fault.

Once we were all transferred over to the *Sea Calf*, we headed home. Billy asked, "So, what is this all about?"

"It's about that dead body we found on the *California Girl* Tuesday morning. And as you know, Dave Smythe owns the boat, and his greasy friend tried to kill us," I said, summing it all up.

"So, what's going on, do you think?" asked Billy.

"How should we know? Smythe killed someone, we know about it, and he wants to kill us too," I said.

"What makes you think that Smythe did it? Just because he owns the *California Girl* doesn't make him the killer," Billy said.

"He ran us off the road with his truck," said Mollie.

"I'm sure he told Mr. Greasy to run us down with his motorboat," added Abigail.

"He surely knows about it all," continued Billy. "He's involved and wants you to back off, but he'll never be sure if you have or not. He probably knows that you've told the harbor master—".

"And the police and the Coast Guard," I interrupted. "He's in trouble and he knows that too."

"But there's no body and no evidence," argued Billy. "He might be able to get away with it whether you all keep quiet or not. That is, if he is the killer."

"But someone's dead and they have to turn up missing eventually," I countered.

"If he were a drifter from somewhere else and no one knew he was here fishing, it's possible that he would never be traced to this town or to the *California Girl*," Billy concluded.

"By the way," I said as casually as possible, "Are you including yourself in this mystery solving process?"

"My brother drinks with Smythe and those other creeps. I can't stand them. Smythe is bad news. I resent him coming down here and dirtying up our town. I'd like to see him get caught for something, but unfortunately there's no law against being a jerk. I'll help you guys."

No one else was talking. I had a feeling that I was

going to be the only Eel Grass Girl and maybe Billy would be an Eel Grass Boy?

"What do you think, Girls?" I asked.

"This is more than I expected. Smythe is going to keep after us until we give up or he kills us. I don't want to pursue this any more! I want out. I don't care what you all do, but I don't want to be involved any-more," whined Abigail.

"Me either," echoed Laura.

"It's not worth it," Mollie chimed in.

"Well, Billy?" I asked.

"I'm in. Maybe you other girls will change your minds after you dry off," said Billy, trying to cheer them up, I guess. It didn't work.

We reached the dock and tied up the *Sea Calf*. Billy went up to the clubhouse with us. We all had our bikes parked there, so we just decided to ride home on our own. We didn't call our parents.

"Don't you want to talk about it?" I asked them.

"There's nothing to talk about," said Mollie. She got on her bike and rode away. I watched her getting smaller and smaller as she rode along the harbor road lined with little shingled cottages and split-rail fences covered with wild roses. Laura and Abigail looked meekly at me and rode off as well. Billy and I went back to sit on the benches overlooking the harbor. I felt really sad. My best friends had just left me to solve this mystery alone. I would rather work with them than with Billy, but what could I do?

# Chapter Thirteen

"What do you think, Billy? You seem to believe that there really was a dead body, don't you?" I asked. Though it was comforting to have someone older to help me, I felt defeated by not having the Eel Grass Girls with me.

"Yes, I believe that there was a body, but I'm not sure Smythe is the killer. He's involved, I'm sure," said Billy. "If only we could find the body!"

"Even if we did, that wouldn't prove who did it. The harbor master suggested that it was just an accident. She even said that the guy might have gotten up and walked away after we saw him! That Jan is weird. I'm sure she's somehow involved," I said.

"You're right," Billy agreed. "She must have driven right past that motorboat. She didn't see it on purpose. She's got to be involved some way."

I wondered what to do next. It was time for Plan A. It was my secret plan. I was tempted to tell Billy, but I was willing to execute it alone.

"What are you going to do now?" asked Billy. He said it in a way which made me think that he was reading my mind.

"I have a crazy plan, but it's the only thing that I can think of to do." I hesitated. Oh well, I might as well tell him, I thought to myself. "When the *California Girl* comes back in, I want to go on board at night and search for clues. Maybe I can find out where Smythe lives and search his house too."

"That's crazy! It's not only crazy, it's *illegal*. The police have to get a warrant to do searches and only when they have some kind of proof that the person is probably guilty. You have no proof, just suspicion. Forget it. I'm not helping you do that! If we got caught, it would be really bad for me. I would lose my jobs!"

"O.K. *O.K.*," I said. "Calm down." I'll just have to do it alone, I told myself. "What bright ideas do you have?"

"I don't know. I'm not used to solving mysteries. It isn't my major in college." I guess that was supposed to be a joke. Billy continued, "If you want help doing anything sensible or reasonable, I'll help you. I think I'd better be getting back to the beach. Have a safe trip home!"

Hey!" I called. "Wait a minute. Can you find out where Smythe and the other crew members live?"

"Breaking and entering isn't my field of studies either," replied Billy. "You are one sick kid." He was looking at me with pitying eyes. I returned his gaze and put all the emotion I could into a pathetic, pleading look.

"Oh, alright," he said. "Go ahead. But if you ge caught, don't say I told you anything," he warned.

Though my Eel Grass Boy was a deserter too, h might be useful yet. Wow! I had lost four co-workers in less than two hours! And I had started out with onl three! O.K. I needed to know when the *California Gir* would return. Then I would need an excuse to get out o the house at night...

# Chapter Fourteen

Friday turned out to be quite interesting. I had wanted to work on the mystery, but a "friend," Rosa, from my school in New York, was vacationing in the area. Her mother and my mother thought it would be "just wonderful" if we all got together and went to the beach. They arrived very early in the morning. We all packed up enough junk to last us a week, stuffed it in our car, and headed for the beach. We went to Lighthouse Beach, just below the lighthouse and Coast Guard station and across from the sandbar where the fishing boat had run aground on Tuesday.

I have to admit that I had fun playing in the surf and building sandcastles with my "buddy." It's not that I can't stand this girl, but we have absolutely nothing in common. We couldn't agree on anything and ended up building separate kingdoms. No problem. It was such a beautiful day, and my Mom doesn't usually take me to this beach. We always go to Mermaid Beach because we can just walk there.

I was thrilled when Mom suggested that we go to the Nor'easter for lunch. Hopefully Billy would be working there. On the way Mom drove by Yacht Harbor Sailing Club to show our guests where I took sailing lessons. My heart leapt when I saw the *California Girl* tied up at her mooring! How long would they stay in port? When would they be going out again? Could I begin Plan A?

We drove back to Main Street and parked behind the Nor'easter. My heart began to pound when I noticed Dave Smythe's red truck also parked in the lot. We would be on the restaurant side so I wouldn't have to see him. But maybe I *would* like to see him and let him know I was still alive.

We entered and got a booth. We ordered chowder and fried clams. I did anyway. My city slicker friend Rosa wanted a hamburger. Her mom told her that she could eat burgers anywhere, but only at the shore could she get fresh seafood. Rosa wouldn't listen. It was just as well, since I didn't want her puking in our car on the way back to the house!

"Why don't you girls go to the ladies' room to wash up?" Mom suggested. Why was it that parents always think children are the only ones with dirty hands? But this was my chance to see if Billy was working. Rosa and I sauntered back toward the passageway connecting the kitchen, restrooms, and bar. I pushed the kitchen door open and saw Billy plunking heaps of salad on little plates.

"Pssst!" I called. He looked up and broke into a wide smile.

"Hey, Nance!" he called back. That was annoying! Nancy Drew was my heroine, but I could get real sick of her name, especially if people use it on me. I should have taken it as a compliment, but it seemed that when people used it, they were making fun of me.

Billy approached me and said in a low voice, "Here are the addresses. I milked them out of my alcoholic brother. Boy, is he a loser! Anyway, if you go down in flames, I'm not going with you." He handed me a folded piece of paper.

"Thanks for the addresses." Thanks for being a real chicken, I wanted to add. How could a guy who had been a teenager only a year or two ago be so timid? It was hard to understand. Yesterday he'd mentioned something about losing his jobs. I wondered if that would really happen. Why did he care so much? His job here was only doing the dirty work around the kitchen. Maybe he really needed the money. Maybe no one would trust him if he got arrested for breaking into someone's house. And I was forgetting that he had to have a good reputation to work at the sailing club.

I wasn't going to get caught, so I didn't have to

worry about that. I was just a kid. They would forgive me even if I did get caught. I would never be sent to jail. Or would I? I pushed those thoughts out of my head. Nancy Drew always did these kinds of things and never got in trouble. I wouldn't either!

"What about Plan A? Hope you've given that one up," he added.

"I just saw the boat back in the harbor. I can't get out tonight, but I plan to go tomorrow night after the band concert."

"You really are sick!" commented Billy. "Who's your friend? Another *Eel*?"

"How do you know about the Eel Grass Girls?" I was shocked. No one knew our secret name, except the four of us.

"I'm not deaf. I've heard you girls talking and giggling. It's no secret," responded Billy.

"Who else knows?" I asked. This was really bad!

"Some of the instructors. We think it's cute. Don't worry," said Billy.

"Billy! Stop yakking and get to WORK!" roared a cook.

"Got to go. Good luck!"

"You never introduced me!" pouted Rosa. "What was all that about? Whose addresses are those?

What are Eel Girls? Why did that man call you sick?"

"Let's go to the ladies' room and I'll explain," I replied.

As we turned, who should walk by on his way to the men's room but Dave Smythe! His face turned almost purple when he saw me. I pulled Rosa into the ladies' room, but Smythe pushed in after us! He grabbed me by my throat with one monstrous hand and pushed me against the wall.

"Look here, Girlie. I never want to see your ugly little face again, understand?" His breath smelled like a garbage can. He was very strong, very angry, and he'd been drinking. He let me go, but I was so scared my legs gave way. I crumpled to the floor. He turned and had trouble opening the door and getting out of the little pink room.

Rosa stood with her mouth open. Big help she was! I got up from the cold damp floor covered with wads of toilet paper and paper towels. We rushed back to our table. Our mothers were blabbing away and took no notice of us. I squeezed myself next to Rosa and filled her in. The restaurant was so noisy no one overheard us, not even our mothers.

"That man was Dave Smythe. I'm investigating him for a crime I believe he committed," I said in a matter-of-fact way, even though my insides felt all mixed up and quivery from being throttled by Dave Smythe. "To answer all your other questions: That man in the kitchen is Billy Jones, one of our sailing instructors at Yacht Harbor. He got me the addresses of that nasty man and the rest of his fishing crew. The Eel Grass Girls are my friends and I. We have a secret—anyway we *thought* it was secret—club which solves mysteries."

"Wow! That is so awesome! A mystery! But are you going to tell your mom about what just happened?" Rosa wanted to know. She looked kind of pale, like she might cry or something.

"Oh, no. She knows the basics of what's going on." I didn't know Rosa well enough to tell her everything. If Billy and the instructors knew our secret name, I might as well tell Rosa. At least she was a girl. But tell Mom about Smythe? I didn't want to create a scene here at the Nor'easter. It wouldn't help our case, I was sure.

"Shouldn't you tell the police or something? He shouldn't go around hurting people that way!" Rosa said.

"Oh, I'm O.K.," I lied. I like to tell the truth, but sometimes it's easier to exaggerate a little. I was still shaking like a recently escaped animal frantically searching for a safe hiding place, but I couldn't let Rosa know that. I wanted to appear "cool," and I didn't want her telling her mother either.

"Could I be an Eel Girl too?" she asked innocently.

"Eel Grass Girl," I corrected. "I would have to ask the other Girls first. Besides, you don't live here. You're staying in another town."

"You don't live here either," she replied. "I can ask my mom to let me stay with you overnight. I know I could solve the mystery."

Rosa wasn't my even friend, but on the other hand my *real* friends had all deserted me. Our food arrived before I could answer her. We ate in silence. It was amazing how the sun and salt water can make a person so hungry.

After lunch I considered asking Rosa to stay over and help me. She was a serious and, I guess, sensible girl. She might make a good Eel Grass Girl. We talked more as we rode home. I told her about the murder and almost getting killed a couple of times. She was so impressed it made me feel supercool. "Cool" was one of my mom's favorite words. I had picked it up, even though kids my age don't use it much.

Back at my house Rosa's mother gathered up all their beach things and packed them into their car. Rosa looked at me to cue me to ask our moms about her staying over. I hesitated.

Then her mom said, "Rosa's grandmother is arriving tonight. We have to get back and set up a cot for her in our cottage."

"Grammy's coming?" screeched Rosa, almost exploding with joy.

"Yes, dear," her mom laughed. "I didn't want you to know until we were sure that she'd be able to make the trip. She called late last night. I guess I should have told you this morning, but I was in such a rush to get here on time, I forgot!"

That solved that problem. Rosa wouldn't be able to stay.

"Sorry I can't stay and help," Rosa said. "You've got to let me know what happens, promise?"

"I promise. Thanks for offering." I guess I had gained a friend, or something. Maybe when I got back to Manhattan I would find that we had more in common than going to the same school and being terrorized by Dave Smythe in a little pink ladies' room!

We said our good-byes as the car backed out of our driveway and headed down our quiet little road. I wouldn't be able to see the other Girls until the next evening. My parents were invited to a party, and they told me they would be out very late, so I had planned my little rendezvous with the *California Girl* at that time.

Because my mom and I were all beached out, we relaxed. Dad was off playing golf. I decided to work on a summer project I actually had been assigned for the summer. I had to collect five special objects to put in a box and decide what I would share about each of them to my new class. I could hardly concentrate, though. I quickly gathered a rock I had found at Mermaid Beach, a pennant I had won for crewing in a Sprite race two weeks ago, a pressed flower from our garden, an acorn from the backyard, and a blue jay feather. I put them into an old cigar box. Assignment completed.

Next I got my black leggings and a navy turtleneck. I put new batteries into one of the flashlights and put it in my backpack. Everything I needed for Plan A!

# Chapter Fifteen

Every Saturday night the Eel Grass Girls met at a certain tree behind the gazebo at the band concert. One of us would bring a blanket and we would listen (and talk) while the music played. It was old people's music, marches and waltzes, but we danced whenever the lights went on around the gazebo, and the audience was invited to come down to dance on the grass. Once in a while the town band would play *The Farmer in the Dell* or some other children's song. We considered the songs too young for us, but that never stopped us from going down and dancing around with the little kids anyway. Plenty of grownups joined in too. We didn't care. It was really fun.

The Eel Grass Girls were quiet on this particular Saturday night. Our parents had dropped us off with countless warnings not talk to strangers or wander away from the park. We sat on Laura's blanket.

"Are you still going to talk to your fisherman friend at church tomorrow?" I asked Laura.

"I suppose so," she replied. "What should I say?"

"Ask him if he knows if there was . . .Oh, I

90

lon't know. It's all so complicated now," I muttered.

"What happened with Billy?" asked Mollie. It was good to see a tiny bit of interest coming back to our group.

"He doesn't want to get in trouble, so he's not going to help me."

"Help you do what?" asked Mollie, sounding downright interested.

"Oh. Plan A. That's all," I said, putting out the bait.

"What is Plan A anyway?" asked Abigail.

"I'm going to search the *California Girl* tonight. I found out that they came in yesterday afternoon."

The Girls stared at me in disbelief.

"You've lost your mind!" exclaimed Laura. "No wonder Billy doesn't want to help you! No one would help you do that!"

"I know. That's why I'm going alone. I don't expect anyone to help." I was having a pity party for myself. Of course I didn't want to go alone, but I didn't want anyone to go with me if they didn't want to.

"When are you going?" asked Abigail. The Girls were acting as if they felt guilty, letting me go alone. Or maybe they were just scared for me.

"After the band concert. Your Dad will take me home. My parents are out at a party. I'm supposed to wait up for them or go to bed, so I'll stuff my pillows

91

under the covers to look like I'm sleeping and then I'll ride my bike down to the harbor. I'll borrow Mollie's dinghy and row out to the *California Girl*. It's as easy as that." I tried to sound confident, but I was really terrified. Excited, but just plain petrified as well.

"What if one of those fishermen is on the boat? What will you do then?" asked Abigail.

"They all have apartments or houses. I found that out too. No one will be there. If anyone is, I'll just jump overboard. They won't be able to find me in the dark water." I sounded braver than I felt.

"How did you find out all this information?" asked Laura.

"Billy," I answered. "He found out where all the crew members live. I'm going to search their houses too, one by one, starting with Smythe."

"First of all," began Mollie, "that's not legal and second, you'd never do any of that by yourself."

"Wait and see," was all I said. No one said anything. Then Laura spoke up.

"I'll ask the fisherman at church if he knows anything about the *California Girl* and Smythe. If he seems to be talkative, I'll ask him about the crew also," she said.

"Great!" I answered. At least someone wanted to do something to help!

*The Farmer and the Dell* began. We left our blanket to join the hordes of little kids and their parents around the gazebo, to act out the song. We formed into small groups with complete strangers. We went through the motions of the song as we all sang out, following the lead of the bandleader, the father of one of Mom's old school friends.

After the lights dimmed, we returned to our blanket, but stood up as *The Star-Spangled Banner* played. The bandleader "God blessed" us, and we went out to the sidewalk on Main Street to wait for Abigail's father. He came along, his Jeep crawling through all the traffic and the dispersing crowds. The girls were so quiet that even Abigail's father suspected that something was wrong.

"You girls still upset by that boating accident?" he asked.

"Yes," we answered, mostly just to answer and not have him pry.

"The harbor master or the police will catch him sooner or later," he asserted.

We didn't believe that even for a minute! Anyway, I was dropped off at my house. All the lights were on, but I knew that no one was home.

"Are you sure you'll be alright? You could stay with us and have your parents pick you up at our house," Abigail's father offered.

"Oh no. I'll be alright. I'm not afraid. I've got the phone, and there are neighbors all around." I got out of the Jeep and walked through the lawn, which was wet with dew.

# Chapter Sixteen

As the Jeep drove away, I ran inside, stuffed my bed full of pillows, changed into my dark outfit, grabbed my backpack, and ran out to hop onto my bike. I pedalled through the dark down Yacht Harbor Road. As I passed the town parking lot next to the pier, I noticed the red truck. Why was it there? Did that mean that Smythe was on the *California Girl*? What should I do?

I decided to row out just to see what he was doing.

I rode on past the club to the shore as far as Mollie's family boathouse. I felt around under the step for the key. Knowing that Smythe was probably on his boat, I was afraid to use my flashlight, even though there was activity in and around the harbor: fishermen, vacationers living on their yachts, and people out to enjoy an evening near the water.

I found the oars and pushed the dinghy down to the water's edge. The heaps of eel grass made it difficult. As I was heaving I felt a big hand clasp my shoulder. My heart leapt into my mouth as I swung around, almost falling into the boat.

"Shhhh!" It was Billy and Mollie and Laura and Abigail!!!

"What are you all doing here?" I asked in a whisper. My heart had settled back into place, and I was filled to overflowing with joy. My friends had not deserted me. They had come to rescue me. They were with me, in more ways than one. I wanted to hug each one of them, but it was too dark—and awkward, know what I mean?

"How did you all get here?" I asked.

"Well," began Billy, "I was coming to rescue you when I saw these three riding their bikes toward the club. I figured that they had had a change of heart about helping you and were on their way here. I piled their bikes into the back of my truck and parked at the club."

"And you?" I asked the Girls.

"We had a quick conference in the backseat of the Jeep after we took you home. We agreed that we couldn't let you do this alone, so we decided to go home, pretend to go to bed, then sneak out and meet at the end of Lowndes River Street and proceed here. So, here we are!" said Abigail. "But," she added, "we don't approve and we think that it's too dangerous."

"You're right about that," I replied, to their surprise. "Did you notice Smythe's truck at the dock?"

"No," was the answer.

"So why are you going out then?" asked Laura.

"I want to know what he's doing out there,

answered. "I'm glad you have on dark clothes. He'll be less apt to see us," I said.

"Yeah," Mollie interjected, "but my boat is white!"

It was true. Her dinghy was gleaming white in spite of the dark night. There was nothing we could do about that. But the moon hadn't risen yet, so we had to get going to take advantage of the darkness.

"Oh, well. Let's push this boat out and hop in. I'll row," offered Billy. "Everyone be quiet."

That was the trouble with letting someone else into our group. Now Billy had made himself the boss and was telling us what to do! I hated that. It was one thing to have Mollie bossing us around because we could ignore her if we wanted to. Someone older was more difficult to ignore. I suppose he was right. We should be quiet. But I resented him telling us that.

We waded through the slimy eel grass, pushing the boat out until it floated, and we could all pile in. Billy put the oars in the oarlocks and pulled on them as quietly as possible. The oars sliced through the still black water. He paused and let us glide between each dip. He was probably doing a better job than we could have done.

As we drifted closer, we could hear voices coming from the *California Girl*. We kept behind other boats which filled the harbor. We could hear Smythe.

"These bales should have come off last night," he was complaining.

"It's not our fault you got drunk and forgot about it," we heard Alex Nickerson say.

"My drinking is none of your business," Smythe retorted.

"I don't want anything to do with your dirty business anymore, anyway!" yelled Alex.

"Keep your voice down! You're in too deep now Nickerson. You've never had any trouble taking your share of the dough, so I don't see why you're griping. I'm helping you make ends meet," he added with a sarcastic sneer.

Alex cursed. We heard someone else grumbling as well.

"O.K. We've got it all. Let's go," ordered Smythe.

At that moment Billy lost one of the oars. It splashed into the water. I lunged for it before it drifted away.

"What was that?" asked Smythe. They paused and listened. We froze.

"Just a fish," said one of the men.

"Those little girls making you jumpy?" asked Alex mockingly.

"Shut up! If it wasn't for you getting so chummy with them, they wouldn't know anything!" yelled Smythe.

"Who's making the noise now?" asked Alex. "I didn't tell them anything. How could they know any hing? You're just paranoid."

"I'm careful, that's what I am. Let's go." They boarded their dory and rowed away into the dark.

"Let's get back and call the police," I whispered.

We rowed hard toward shore, confident that they wouldn't hear us while they were talking and rowing in another direction.

"What do you think is in those bundles?" asked Mollie.

"I don't know, but it must be something bad," answered Laura.

"How do we know it is? Maybe it's just dead fish or equipment," argued Abigail, the lawyer's daughter.

"They're unloading at night, two days after they returned to port. It's not fish. Why would they sneak out here at night to unload equipment? It's something illegal," said Billy. "I knew that guy Smythe was a creep!"

We ran into the shore and dragged the dinghy above the high tide mark and put the oars away. I grabbed my bike, and we rushed to the club. Billy stuck my bike in the back of his truck along with the others.

"Let's sneak down to the parking lot and see what they do," I suggested. We crept down to the town pier and dodged behind crates so we could see Smythe coming in, but he was nowhere in sight! We didn't hear him rowing or arguing with his crew. Nothing. Only some distant music from a party somewhere over on Deer Island.

"That's strange," uttered Mollie.

"To say the least," added Billy. "Where did they go?

"Maybe they heard us and are waiting for us to leave," I suggested.

"They didn't hear us. Let's go get the police or the Coast Guard, someone, before they get away," said Mollie.

"They've already gotten away," said Laura. She'd had enough. "Let's go home before we all get into trouble."

"No! Billy, get your truck," I pleaded. "Let's drive over to Deer Island Road and look for them. They must be there on the shore."

"Or maybe they've got another truck over on the road, or anywhere in between," said Billy. "You all game?"

"O.K.," said the Girls, with a bit of their old spark.

We piled into Billy's truck, five on the seat. Not exactly legal, but this was an emergency. We bounced down the hill to Lowndes River Street. At the lighthouse we turned right again toward the island. Deer Island wasn't really an island, but a peninsula with a long dark road leading to it. The harbor was on the right, and the bay in front of the lighthouse was on the left.

It was here that we thought we might intercept Smythe and his crew, but no one was around. We did see

ome cars and trucks parked, but Billy didn't recognize
ny of them as belonging to Smythe's gang. I guessed they
elonged to some fishermen who believed that fish bite
nore at night, or that the tide was perfect for catching a
keeper," that is, a fish that is the legal size to keep. My
ad says that the fishing laws have caused the striped bass
o become more plentiful, but he still can't seem to catch
ne. Most of the cars were from out of state.

"Let's go onto the island and look," I directed Billy.

"Wait a minute. I don't want to meet Smythe on
ne of those narrow roads," protested Billy.

"Come on," I begged. "They're going to get away!"

"They can't get away," he assured me. "If they're on
he island, this is the only road going on or off. They'll
ave to pass by us. Why don't two of you go down to the
each and see if you can hear or see anything?"

Abigail and I walked down to the shore and lis-
ened while Billy turned the truck around and waited. He
hut the lights off. We couldn't see or hear anything but
he distant music. All of a sudden we saw headlights
pproaching from the island. We raced back to Billy's
ruck and jumped in.

"Someone's coming! It might be them." We
aited. A blue truck passed. It looked like three men in
he cab. The back was covered with a tarp.

"Follow them!" I ordered.

"Hey! Wait a minute!," Billy protested. "We can't just follow them. They'll notice us."

"They're getting away. Just follow. We've got to see where they're going."

We started up slowly and cruised along, with the distance between our truck and theirs growing steadily. They drove right through town and then south along the main road to Muddy River. When they turned onto Uncle Willy's Lane, we drove on past, turned around and came back. Billy pulled into the parking lot of Patsy's Pie Shoppe, just north of Uncle Willy's Lane.

"I'm not going in there!" announced Billy.

"O.K., then we will. Let's get our bikes, Girls," I said.

"Do we all have to go?" asked Abigail.

I was already getting my bike out. Mollie was beside me, and Billy helped her get hers out. In silence we rode down the lane. I didn't blame the others for not coming. At least I had one other Eel Grass Girl to go with me.

After what seemed like two miles, we came upon a little cottage where several trucks, including the blue one, were parked. The "gang" was unloading whatever it was. That was enough for me. We rode back, and Billy helped us put our bikes back in his truck.

"Let's go to the police," said Mollie.

"Maybe the Coast Guard would be better," I said, remembering Officer Personality.

"They don't work on land," said Billy. "Anyway, I don't think they do."

"But what if something starts on the water and ends in town? Can they help then?" I asked.

"I don't know," replied Billy. "You girls should go home. That I do know!"

"Not now!" hollered Mollie, almost breaking our eardrums. "Those creeps can be caught right now. We can't let them get away."

"But we don't even know for sure what it is they've got," said Billy.

"You know it's got to be bad. Maybe it's drugs," whispered Laura, finally saying something.

Billy drove us to the police station. Our favorite police officer was on duty.

"Excuse me, sir," I began, too late to realize that 'sir' didn't apply to female officers. "We . . .uh . . .think someone has some drugs."

She looked a little bit interested.

"Location?" she asked.

"Uncle Willy's Road. First cottage, way down on the left. There are three trucks out front. The blue truck made the delivery."

"Proof?"

"We saw them unloading a fishing boat and then taking the packages to the cottage," I said.

The officer looked at Billy, as if to ask him to verify our story.

"It's true," he said. "We don't know exactly what they've got, but we think it might be drugs since they unloaded it at night."

She radioed someone and asked whoever it was to come to the station.

To our dismay, two "rent-a-cops" drove up a few minutes later. They were young officers, working only during the summer season at our resort town. They didn't even carry guns!

"Drug bust on Uncle Willy's Road," she informed the officers, who were as shocked as we were disappointed. She gave them all the information.

"But they might have guns!" exclaimed Mollie. "Don't you have any real police who can go?"

Officer Personality glowered at us. "Identities?"

Did she mean ours or theirs? "Dave Smythe the fisherman, Alex Nickerson, and one other," I told her. The officers drove off. That was that.

Billy took me home first. I thanked them all profusely. It meant so much to me that they had taken the risk to join me in Plan A. They were all true to our Eel Grass creed. We had done the right thing. Those crooks would get caught, and the dead man would be avenged.

I quietly unloaded my bike and gently leaned it against the side of my house. I crept in through my window and snuggled down into my soft bed for a peaceful sleep.

# Chapter Seventeen

"Breakfast!"

What a refreshing sleep I had had. I popped out of bed and gave my parents a cheery "Good morning."

"Well," said Dad, "I can't remember ever seeing you so cheerful so early in the morning."

"I feel great!" was all I could say.

We got ready for church and drove all the way to Muddy River to a little white church. The service was short and sweet. I kept wondering how the drug bust had gone. There was no way I could escape my family on a Sunday to go down to the police station to find out. I would have to wait until Monday . . .

At church someone asked us to a cookout. Everyone at church was invited, so we decided to go home and change, whip up a salad, then meet the others at a house near one of the freshwater ponds. It would be fun.

When we got there, I looked for some of the kids. We had started down to the pond when someone called my name. I turned to see a man with a long graying braid hanging down his back. He was a regular at our church. I had heard that he was a local Native American.

He was talking to my parents.

"Saw you sailing on Thursday. You do more goofing off than real sailing, it seems." He was smiling, but I didn't like his comment.

"I didn't see you," I answered.

"I was in a motorboat near the beach inside the cut."

"Were you fishing?" I asked not really caring.

"No. I'm the assistant shellfish warden," he replied.

"Oh," I uttered. I waved good-bye to my parents and turned to go on down to the pond. Some people are weird, no doubt about it! Then it occurred to me that he must have been there just before our accident in the *Minnow*, but I didn't want to discuss it with him. What did it matter?

The cookout was fun. Afterwards we drove home. I felt satisfied and good. Full of yummy food and exhausted from lots of swimming and running around. I just love that summer kind of feeling. Now I looked forward to lying on my bed, reading some comics, and thinking of nothing.

Mom checked the messages on the answering machine. Her friend Sherry had called. She sounded terrible and asked Mom to come over right away.

"Muffy, will you come with me?" she asked.

"I guess so," I replied. All I wanted to do was lie down and have some quiet time to myself, but Mom always said that Sunday should be dedicated to God and to helping others. How could I say "no"?

We walked to Sherry's house. It was just down the road. No one answered the door, so we walked in. The house looked dark and deserted.

"Sherry?" Mom called. A slight murmur came from the bedroom. Mom rushed in first. Sherry was in bed and looked terrible.

"Oh Sherry!" she exclaimed. "Whatever has happened to you?"

"We went to Mac's Fish House last night for dinner," she said weakly. "Food poisoning, I think."

"You're going to the doctor!" Mom announced.

"No, no. I'll be alright. Just get me a soda from the kitchen."

I ran to the kitchen and brought back a glass of ginger ale, which Sherry gulped down.

"What did you eat?" asked Mom.

"Littlenecks," replied Sherry. Littlenecks are small quahogs, eaten raw on the half shell.

"They must have been tainted!" said Mom. "Did you call Mac's?"

"No, I couldn't." Mom got on the phone and called Mac's. The owner apologized. I'm sure he didn't want to be sued for poisoning his customer. He did admit that other people had reported stomach problems. Mom asked him where he got his shellfish. Then she hung up.

"He gets his shellfish from either of two shellfishermen, Janie Eldredge or Larry Knowles. I'm going to call the shellfish warden right now," said Mom. And she did.

Did she say Larry Knowles? What a coincidence. A fisherman and a shellfisherman in his spare time. Was he the culprit?

Mom was just finishing up with her phone call to the warden. "I left a message. He doesn't work on Sunday," she said.

"Why don't you call that assistant warden who was at the cookout?" I asked.

"Would you call, dear? His name is Pierce Maker. He might still be at the party. Call there first, then try his home. His name should be in the book."

I called the house where the party had been. He had already left, so I looked up his phone number and dialed.

"Hi," I greeted him when he answered. "This is Mora Cortez. You met me at the cookout this afternoon," I reminded him. I guess he didn't remember. "You were talking to my parents and you made a remark about my sailing." There was a pause. He seemed a little dense. I wondered if I could I get any information from this guy.

"Oh. . .yeah," he said, finally.

"I need some information on a shellfisherman named Larry Knowles," I said.

"He's not a shellfisherman. He fishes on the *California Girl*," he replied.

"But he's been selling littlenecks to Mac's Fish House," I said.

"Really? Are you sure?" he sounded very surprised.

"That's what Mac said," I stated. "What's so strange about that?"

"Oh, no law against selling shellfish, but I've never seen him do it and wouldn't think he had the time or would need the money since he's got a steady fishing gig."

"To change the subject a little, what would make a quahog so bad that it would make someone sick?" I asked.

"Well, it could be old or have some sort of Red Tide. You've heard about that, haven't you?" I nodded my head, even though he couldn't see me. Some sort of weird something that grows in the sea and gets into fish and shellfish.

"Or if the shell was scratched in bad water," he finished.

"What?" I asked, not very politely.

"Some of the beds have to be closed when the water gets polluted, usually from cesspools leaching down into he water around a marsh and flowing out into the beds. Crocker Pond and Duck Creek, for instance. Those beds have been productive for hundreds of years, but now the hells can't be harvested."

"Could someone fish there and get away with t?" I asked.

"It's posted that the beds are closed. The only way hey could do it is if they fished at night," he laughed. "And that would be pretty hard."

I thanked him and quietly hung up the phone. Mom was talking to Sherry and not paying any attention o me. I took out my pad of paper where I had copied the addresses of all the fishermen. Knowles lived on Duck Creek Road! Could it be that he scratched tainted clams at night? But why? It didn't make sense.

"You had better rest now, Sherry," Mom was saying. "I'll stop by later to check in on you and see if you need anything. Call if you feel worse."

Mom asked me to bring in the whole bottle of ginger le and some soda crackers. Then we left.

"What did you find out?" asked Mom. I told her about the fisherman.

"Well, I know Janie," she said. "She was a few years behind me in school. She would never sell bad clams to anyone. Never!"

I asked Mom a few questions about clams being quahogs, but she said it was the other way around Quahogs are hard-shell clams. Whatever.

Now I had more information, but I didn't know how all the clues fit together. I needed to meet with the Girls.

# Chapter Eighteen

'Emergency meeting tomorrow at the bandstand at noon," I told Laura.

"But it's supposed to rain," she whined.

"So what? We can stand in the center of the gazebo and we won't get wet," I countered.

"But how do we get there? I'm not riding my bike in the rain!"

"Fine!" I was angry. Why was she being such a wimp?

"I'm sorry," I apologized. "We have to meet somewhere."

"Let's ask Abigail to invite us for lunch. Our parents can drop us off. And it's near town so if it clears, we can walk to the Nor'easter," she suggested.

"Why go to the Nor'easter?' I asked.

"I know you want to talk to Billy Boy," she teased.

"I do," I admitted, "and I want to find out from the police if they caught Smythe and the gang. I'm sure they did."

I called Abigail. She agreed to invite us all for lunch. As it turned out, Monday was a bright and beautiful day. We decided to ride our bikes to her house. After we ate, we swapped stories about how we got back into bed on Saturday night without waking our parents. Then we walked to town to the Nor'easter.

Billy wasn't there, but as we walked by the alleyway leading to the parking lot, we saw him talking to a red-faced man who looked very much like him. His brother maybe? Anyway, when they saw us, the man gave us a look that made us feel very uncomfortable. We paused. Billy looked at us in a strange way, so we walked on.

"I wonder what that's all about," said Mollie. "Do you think that's his brother?"

"Probably. He looks like him. Billy's been asking him a lot about Smythe and his crew. Since his brother's friends with Smythe, maybe Smythe's become suspicious. And we'll have to wait until sailing class tomorrow to find out!" complained Laura.

We discussed many possibilities. I filled them in on Sherry's shellfish poisoning. We couldn't figure out how it fit in with the rest of the mystery or if it even did at all.

"Did you find out anything from the fisherman at your church?" Abigail asked Laura. How had we forgotten to ask her?

"He said that Smythe has a bad reputation. It's not only because he's not a Cape Codder that people don't like him, but because he's a bully. That isn't exactly how he said it, but I think that's what he meant. He said that

Knowles is also from somewhere around Boston. From Wallington. He didn't know anything else and I didn't know what to ask," she said. "I'm not as clever as Muffy and Mollie."

"Sure you are," I encouraged her. "You did a good job." But I wondered what good was more useless information. We ambled along toward the police station, our second stop. When we arrived, we were thrilled to see the police chief standing at the front desk, drinking coffee with Officer Personality. For once we wouldn't have to deal with her alone.

"What have we here?" he asked in a friendly manner.

"We want to know how the drug bust went last Saturday night," Mollie blurted out.

"Oh. So *you* were involved in that?" he asked, not smiling any more.

"Yes. Why?" I asked.

"You see, we had a bad car accident that night. All the regular officers were helping out. Someone had a little too much to drink and drove into someone else's living room. A few minor injuries, so the kids, I mean two of our temporary officers, were the only ones available to check your story out," he explained. He cleared his throat.

"You gave the information?" he asked, looking at us inquisitively.

"Yes," we nodded in anticipation.

He leaned over into the office space, took a clip-board from a desk, and flipped through some of the pages clipped to it.

"First cottage down on the left of Uncle Willy's Lane? Lots of trucks? Dave Smythe and Alex Nickerson there?" Why did I have such a bad feeling about this?

"Yes," we answered again.

"Nothing. *Nada. Rien du tout.*" Ohhhh. He was a linguist! But his message was confusing.

"That couldn't be, sir," I began. "We followed them there. We saw them unloading the packages."

"How was it that you were following them?" he asked. We explained about the murder, rowing out to the boat, and following Smythe's truck.

"How did you follow him without him noticing you?" he wanted to know. We explained about Billy's truck and the bikes.

"Don't you kids have a curfew?" he asked, changing the subject. Our looks of "please don't ask" persuaded him to continue.

"By the time my men arrived at the scene, it was deserted. No men. No trucks. No drugs."

"Don't you have a drug-sniffing dog?" asked Abigail.

"We could get one sent down here, but we don't

have enough to go on," he was saying. I just couldn't believe him. Did we have to solve this whole case ourselves? We had been the invincible Eel Grass Girls, but we felt like limp noodles now. Anyway, I did. We were so close, yet so far away. So many clues, but no solution.

"Well, thank you," I said. Laura and Abigail were staring blankly. Mollie was steaming mad, I could tell.

"Thanks for nothing," she muttered under her breath.

We walked back down Main Street in silence. Then finally Laura spoke up. "I don't get it."

"Get what?" asked Abigail.

"This whole thing. Is it about drugs or murder or rotten clams?"

"It might be everything. Either they're all connected or they're separate mysteries," said Abigail. I had no bright ideas.

As we approached the Nor'easter, Mollie said, "I'm going in there. Billy owes us an explanation."

"An explanation for what?" I asked.

"For that weird look he gave us," she said as she stormed into the restaurant. The rest of us sat down on a bench in front and waited. After a while she came out.

"Wait 'til you hear what he told me!" she said. She motioned us to follow her down the street. We walked back to Abigail's as she filled us in.

"Billy's brother knows that something is up with Smythe, but he doesn't know exactly what. He doesn't want to know. He knows that Billy has been asking a lot of questions about Smythe and his gang. And he knows that Billy knows us and that Smythe is annoyed with us for snooping around. He's afraid that Smythe might be dangerous which we already know. He wants Billy to back off and stay away from us and tell us to stay away from everyone!"

Wow! I guess we have to be really careful now. Though I didn't know how. Because it was a small town we kids were allowed to be on our own, most of the time. It was supposed to be a safe place.

"And that's not all," Mollie continued. "Even though Symthe wasn't there when the cops came, he found out about it. It seems that he has a friend who lives in that little dark cottage across the street, on Uncle Willy's, and the friend woke up when the truck pulled in and everyone started talking. He saw us on our bikes and heard the cops come later and told Smythe everything and boy is he mad!"

That bit of news sent shivers down our spines. He was apt to get really ugly now. What were we going to do?

"Billy's brother doesn't seem to know about the murder or the drugs so Billy didn't tell him. No one seems to know about the murder except the murderer and us and the people we've told! The brother has no idea why we are snooping, so Billy told him that we're just dumb kids!" said Mollie.

We were too shocked to be mad about the "dumb kids" part. Now Smythe knew that we knew about the drugs too, if that's what they were. We had to watch our backs now, as the gangsters say.

Back at Abigail's we went swimming in Snow Pond and tried to have some fun, but a gloomy feeling hung in the air. We played around her yard until it was time to go home. We had ridden our bikes over, but now we were afraid to split up and ride home.

"Laura and Mollie can go together, but you'll have to go alone, Muffy," said Abigail.

"I'll ride with my head on backwards and I'll be alright," I laughed, not feeling very confident. A red or blue or any-colored truck could come out of nowhere and run me over. Even though it was the crowded summer season at the shore, no one would probably see it. I almost called my mom to come and get me, but I had no reason. No reason, that is, that I could tell my mom about . . .

# Chapter Nineteen

I said good-bye to the girls. I started home alone. Although I told myself to be careful, my thoughts began to churn. I wanted to talk to Billy. I wanted to talk to the police chief, though I wasn't sure if that would help. I wanted to talk to the Coast Guard. The station was right there, so I thought I might as well go in. I turned off the road at the lighthouse and entered the old station. My friend, the petty officer, was with Pete. He questioned me with his eyes.

"May I talk to you?" I asked. He led me into a little office filled with photos of the old "Lifesavers," their dories and horses, ropes and stations. The Coast Guard was still mainly involved with pulling people out of the water.

He was still looking at me. Waiting for me to begin. I poured out my heart to him, giving him all the information, all the details, all my suspicions and questions, all my fears. I hadn't planned on doing this, but it just rushed out. He listened.

"We could do a thorough search of the boat, but probably wouldn't find anything now. If we could get a 'sniffer' down here, I mean a drug-sniffing dog, he could ell us if there had been drugs on board, but even that may not be enough. If we had an identity for the dead man, it would help us. I don't know how the shellfishing thing is connected. It might be something or nothing."

He hadn't said anything astounding, but he was on my side. I could tell.

"Keep me posted on anything you find out. We'll keep an eye on that boat. I have to tell you that we've heard some rumors. Drugs are coming into town, we know, but no one knows how. The authorities are baffled. This may be the answer." He believed me, and he was treating me like an real person! It made me feel great. The officer was seeing the big picture, as they say. There was hope that the clues would fit together somehow. I pedalled home, almost forgetting about danger.

As I rode I began mulling the whole mystery over again in my mind. At the next hill, I didn't have the strength to pedal up, so I hopped off my bike and began to push it up the hill.

"Hello little sister." I turned to see Alex Nickerson looming over me. I know I turned white as a sheet as I stared up into his face. My whole life flashed before my eyes. Where were all those annoying tourists now? The road was completely deserted. Even with all the new building going on in town, I was on a hill surrounded by forests of pines and oaks.

"I am going to die. I am going to die," I said over and over to myself. I could throw my bike at him and run or scream, but I couldn't get away from a big guy like him.

"So, tell me all you know," he demanded. I didn't think I could lie. That would anger him more. But my dad always says that in a card game, you don't let the other players see what cards you have in your hand. I couldn't tell all. I had to think fast.

"I know that you all unloaded something from your boat and took it to a cottage on Uncle Willy's Lane. And I know about the murder."

Now it was Alex who looked shocked. "What murder?"

"You don't know?" I asked, never imagining that he wouldn't know.

"My friends and I saw a dead body on your boat," I said.

"A young, dark-haired guy?"

"Yes."

"Smythe said he quit! That liar. I'm through with Smythe. He's gone too far! Even if I get sent up the river I don't care. I can't live like this any longer!" He turned and walked quickly through the woods.

I raced up the hill and didn't stop until I was safely home. How had Alex just popped out of the woods like that while I was going up that hill? It finally occurred to ne that Shell Road, where Alex lived, was just on the other side of that wood. A little general store, down the street a way, was where he was probably headed to buy cigarettes or something.

# Chapter Twenty

Back at home I found my parents sitting at the kitchen table. Mom was knitting, and Dad was reading the local paper. They greeted me as I came in and asked me how my day was. I gave a quick answer.

"What does 'getting sent up the river' mean?" I asked.

"It means going to jail," answered my dad without looking up from his paper.

Dad kept on reading and I found a snack to eat, then sat down with them. I was still shaking from my encounter with Alex. Why was he talking about going to jail? My parents didn't seem curious about my question. It was just as well. Was Alex going to turn himself in to the police? Wow! If he did, then Smythe would have to get caught.

I asked Mom how Sherry was doing. She was still a little weak but much better.

"Why doesn't that woman go back to Wallington?" Dad burst out.

"What woman, dear?" asked Mom.

"That harbor master. She doesn't know anything about anything, coming from so far inland. She probably never saw water until she moved here two years ago. Why an't they get anyone local to take these positions?" he asked.

"Someone like you?" she asked, her eyes laughing
t him. "You grew up near Manila Bay so I'm sure you
ould do a better job."

"You know what I mean," he grumbled.

"What you mean is that you don't like what she did
nd you don't want to blame it on her being a woman, so
ou blame it on the town where she was raised."

Wallington. Wasn't it strange that Larry Knowles
nd Jan the harbor master were both from the same
own? And Larry worked for Smythe, and Jan didn't see
ne boat that almost killed us?

I couldn't wait to tell the Girls, but I would have to
ait for sailing class the next day. When I got up from the
ible Mom said "Honey" in a way that made me nervous,
You're working on a fisherman mystery, aren't you?"
low, what was I supposed to say to that?

"Oh. You mean that dead body thing?" I asked as
nnocently as possible.

"Yes. That thing."

"Kind of. Because there's no body, there's not
eally much to do about it," I said.

"I'm asking because I need your help. Today when I
necked in on Sherry she told me that her sister's neighbor's
iece arrived looking for a missing boyfriend. The girl says

that he came to the shore for a summer fishing job. Sh
hasn't heard from him in a while and is worried.

"He was an irresponsible sort of person so everyon
is telling her that he's just wandered off somewhere, but sh
insists that he'd changed and he'd found a good job here
She said he was staying somewhere temporarily and com
municated only by phone—pay phone—so his calls can't b
traced to an address. I wouldn't want to get her all upset
but do you think that he could be the one you found?"

Mom looked kind of sad. I wanted to cry
Someone's boyfriend, a person who'd recently turned hi
life around. Now that the body had an identity, his deat
took on new meaning, if he were the one.

"Does she have a picture?" I asked.

"Most likely," said Mom. "I'll call Sherry and ge
in touch with her sister."

Mom went to the phone and made a couple of calls

"O.K. Let's go. Want to come, dear?" she asked Dad

"Oh no. I'll just stay here and keep the fires burn
ing," he said. Whatever that means!

Sherry's sister lived on a back road leading t
Muddy River. She came out to greet us and led u
through the pines to her neighbor's house. The neighbo
was also waiting for us and came out with a wispy-lookin
young woman with long, stringy, taffy-colored fair. Th

126

eighbor was big and wore no makeup, yet her gray hair as wound around pink plastic curlers. She seemed tense, nd the girl had a vacant look in her gray eyes. We sat at a edwood picnic table under white pine trees, their soft, llen needles covering the ground.

"What was your boyfriend's name?" I asked, too te to realize that I should have said "is."

"Jake," was the girl's answer. Her eyes now ocused on me. "Here's his picture." She stuck a photo nder my nose.

I wished that I could have fainted. I guess that at's what females did in the olden days so they wouldn't ave to deal with a bad situation. I had fainted on the shing boat, but now I couldn't do it. Instead I began to ry. That started it. The girl began to sob, and we all five f us just sat there at the wooden table and cried. Finally, e big neighbor went inside and brought out a box of ssues. We all blew our noses and got to work.

"He's the one I saw on the boat. I'm sure he's ead," I said. The girl stifled another sob. I felt so sad for er, but I was thankful she came to find her boyfriend. ow we knew who the dead man was!

"Let's go to the police," said the neighbor. We l piled into our car. My mom had decided that she ould drive.

At the station, Officer Personality told us that the chief was busy. We ought to come back later, she suggested. My mom let her know that we weren't leaving and that what we had to say was important. Because there were no chairs, we just stood and looked around. I gave the officer an evil stare, hoping she would see me, but she never looked up from her desk.

Finally a door opened. The police chief came out leading Alex Nickerson in handcuffs! My mouth fell open and I stared in disbelief.

"Hi, little sis!" he greeted me, to everyone's surprise, including my own. "I feel like a new man. Thanks for the tip." He winked at me as he was escorted down hall. Everyone was now staring at me.

"What was that about?" asked Mom. I just shrugged.

In a few minutes the chief returned and asked us into his office.

He had at least two chairs. We let the neighbor and her niece have them. We told him about Jake.

"Alex told me. We're going to bring Smythe in. Tell me exactly what happened when you found the body," said the chief.

I went through all the information again. He took notes. Then he turned to the niece. "Don't worry. We'll find the killer, and we'll bust them all for this drug running."

"So it was drugs in those bundles?" I asked, feeling indicated.

"Yep. Already have a call into the Coast Guard. Not a word of this to anyone, you hear?" He gave us a very stern look. We all nodded "yes."

The niece began crying again, so we left and drove them back home. When Mom and I got home, we saw Billy's truck and found him talking to my dad.

"Billy stopped by to bring you your lunch bag," my dad told me, holding up the bag. I had left it at the club, but who cares? Because Billy obviously had some information, I had to forgive his earlier weirdness and calling us "dumb." My parents went inside and left us to talk. We walked over to his truck, parked on the street.

"The *California Girl* is going out again," he told me. "They shouldn't be getting away with this. Even my brother is avoiding them. I think he's actually going to stop drinking! It's getting him nowhere fast!"

"Let me tell you what's happened." I filled him in on my conversation with the Coast Guard officer, the Wallington connection of Knowles and the harbor master, and Jake. I left out the part about Alex Nickerson and the Coast Guard closing in on the gang. Since we didn't know what to do next, we decided to talk after sailing school. Maybe it would all be over soon anyway.

# Chapter Twenty-One

The next day the Girls and I met on the deck at the yacht club. It was a gray day. The breeze was a little stiff. Some of the kids were nervously asking instructors if we were really going out. I noticed that the *California Girl* was still at her mooring. I was bursting with impatience to tell the Girls about Jake, but I couldn't mention Alex. There was no privacy in our little cottage, so phone calls were impossible.

After the opening meeting, we filed down the wooden stairs to the beach. Because the *Minnow* was still at the boat doctor, we chose a blue Sprite, named the *Salt Quahog*. We were supposed to practice racing starts. We had trouble getting out from between the piers, as usual, but finally did it.

When we sailed near the *California Girl*, I was shocked to see Alex Nickerson on board! How did he get there? The last time I saw him he was in handcuffs, presumably going to jail. He had confessed. How could they let him go again? That police chief must be crazy, I thought. And I couldn't even talk to the Girls about it, but I could tell them everything else.

"Let's get away from that boat!" hissed Laura

I don't trust those guys. They might have a gun on board and try to shoot us."

"They wouldn't dare," whispered Mollie, forever the know-it-all. But I was sure she was right.

The whole gang was there, including Knowles, Mr. Rotten Clam." I told the Girls all about that and about Jake, my visit to the Coast Guard, and the Wallington connection.

"You've been busy!" Abigail exclaimed. "Why does everything happen to you?"

"I don't know," I said. "I wish that you could share more of my daily trauma!"

We also noticed Joe and an officer puttering around a Coast Guard vessel at the town pier. Not the kiddie pool one, but a bigger craft. I had never seen it here before. It was usually moored over at the fish pier.

The racing starts went just fine. The *Sea Cow* formed one end of the starting line, and a big orange ball was the other. The air horn would blow to let us know how many minutes we had left before the actual start: three, two, one and a half, one, thirty seconds, twenty, ten, three, two, one, start!

We were first over a few times, but had to protest some of the boys for hitting us with their boat. They counterprotested us, but of course they were at fault. We tied a red ribbon, our protest "flag," to one of our stays. After we got back to the club, we had a mock protest meeting and fought it out. Mr. Prince said that we were in the right and if it had been a real race, the boys would have been thrown out of the race. We knew that!

As we sat on the deck, we saw the *California Girl* chugging out to the sound and to the ocean beyond. I glanced over at the Coast Guard boat. Joe and the officer were watching. Then Joe called someone on the radio. Was something going on? Probably, but I was too dumb to figure it out.

We went to the Clam Bar for lunch after class was over. Billy had an instructors' meeting with Mr. Prince and couldn't get away. We sat on the riverbank and ate. It felt good to have nothing to mull over. The police were really working on the case now and had notified the Coast Guard. The *California Girl* was on its way out to sea. No one could harm us now. Just then I heard a crack, and something flew by my head. It was Mr. Greasy in a boat, with a shotgun pointed straight at us!

"Duck!" I shrieked. We hit the grass, but we were still completely exposed. He was just a few yards from us. He could easily shoot us one by one. People fishing on the bridge began to scream and run in all directions. Mr. Greasy sped into Snow Pond and disappeared.

"We've got to catch him!" yelled Mollie, breathlessly. Abigail, you and Laura ride to your grammy's house. See if ou can see where he moors his boat. He probably has a car arked somewhere. And call the police!"

Mollie and I rushed across the street and along the iverbank where it opened up into the pond. A tangle of oats filled the small pond. It was little more than a parking lot for boats. My mom had told me she swam there as child, but not now because it wasn't the same. Not as ice, as I well knew. Especially now.

We saw some movement down on the right, near vhere Abigail's grandmother lived. There were several ittle lanes going down to the pond on that side. He could ave parked on any one of them. I hoped that Abigail and Laura would get there in time.

We ran back to our bikes, stepping over our lunch prawled all over the grass, and rode with all our might fter Laura and Abigail.

When we reached the grammy's house, we found he girls hiding down at the beach.

"See. He's tying up his boat. What a creep. He hinks he's getting away with this!" said Laura.

"The police are on their way," said Abigail. We vaited. We watched him row his dinghy to shore and move p the beach. It was high tide, so the beach was narrow,

and he had to dodge heaps of eel grass and little pools o
incoming water.

We heard a distant siren. "They're not using a siren
are they?" I asked, listening to it approach. "What idiots!

Mollie leapt down the embankment to follow th
man. Abigail and Laura ran to the end of the driveway t
meet the police cruiser. I followed a path through th
brush which connected the yard to the nearest lane. I sa
Mollie running up the lane toward me.

"He's on a bike! Quick!"

We ran to the end of the lane as the cruiser entered

"No, no!" yelled Mollie. "He's on a bike. Tha
way!" She waved her hand toward the street. The cruise
backed up and raced down the narrow street. We split up
each taking a different direction. We ran trying to catch
sight of Mr. Greasy or head him off, but he'd disap
peared! Mollie was sure that he'd gone to the left, but w
couldn't find him. The cruiser circled around an
around. Greasy was gone.

I was standing on Cod Lane when I saw a move
ment on Maple Street. I dodged through a yard an
under a clothesline hung with fresh-smelling new wash
Those bright white sheets and undershirts might shiel
me from Greasy's dark and evil stare.

I caught a glimpse of him sneaking into a tumbled

own shack among some outbuildings of a vacant home. All the buildings on the lot were in disrepair. Most likely someone from the Midwest owned the property, hadn't used it for years, but couldn't bear to sell it. Mr. Greasy hadn't seen me, so I ran back under the clothesline to the top of Cod Lane where the other girls were talking to the policeman.

"He's in one of those outbuildings behind that rundown house on Maple Street. He has a gun, so maybe you need backup," I knew that's what they say in the movies. It sounded good to me.

The policeman radioed the station, and before long I heard another siren! These guys should watch more television. Then maybe they'd know that they were supposed to sneak up on the bad guys, not scare them away!

They surrounded the little shack. The Girls and I hid behind the clothesline house, out of the way of flying bullets. Our man came out with his hands up, when asked to, and they handcuffed him and put him, his bike, and his gun into one of the cruisers. We wanted to gloat, but I didn't think that would help anything. This man had tried to kill us twice. It was better for us to keep out of sight.

After the cruiser left with Greasy, we approached the car that was left. It was the officer who had first arrived.

"I radioed the harbor master to check out that boat. Hop in and we'll drive down to the water." We did

as he said and drove the short distance to the shore. W
told him about the incident last week and suggested tha
it may be the same boat Mr. Greasy used to run us down
The harbor master was approaching. She checked th
boat, then met us at the end of Abigail's dock.

"Know who owns the boat?" asked the officer.

"I'm not sure," she said.

"Can't you find out from that number on th
front of it?" asked Laura.

"We can do that," said the officer. "And check th
hull to see if it could have been the same boat that ra
into these young ladies last week."

We walked back to the cruiser with him. He fille
out a report and asked us if we were sure that we wer
alright. He thanked me for giving him the tip whicl
helped him nab Mr. Greasy, and we thanked him fo
coming. Then he drove off.

"What a day!" exclaimed Laura.

"I've had enough!" said Abigail. "Let's go back t
my house and eat," she suggested. "We never finished ou
lunch. By now the seagulls must have eaten what we left o
the riverbank."

"Sure!" We went back to Abigail's and ate. W
talked about the capture of Mr. Greasy and wondere
how the police would get Smythe. I wanted to tell ther

everything, but I couldn't. It's not a good feeling to keep a secret from your best friends, but what could I do? I had promised the police chief not to tell about the police working with the Coast Guard, even though I didn't really know what was going on.

We celebrated by making sundaes. It was a sweet ending to a bitter mystery. We congratulated each other on our bravery. We *were* brave. We were the old invincible Eel Grass Girls again! We couldn't even be shot at close range, we boasted. We felt great.

After we finished our ice cream, I wanted to go home and rest. Now that we were finally safe, I felt tired. I hoped that there were no more bad guys we'd forgotten about. We had assumed that our greasy friend had left town. Boy, were we wrong! I said good-bye and pedalled off.

# Chapter Twenty-Two

It was a long trip home. All the excitement had zapped my usual limitless energy. Riding by the Coast Guard Station, I decided to stop and to talk to my friend again.

"We've got them now!" he said as he welcomed me into his office. "We sent our big cutter out and some bigger craft met them. We got the *California Girl* out at the fishing bank while she was meeting her supplier. That Alex Nickerson helped us set it up. He's working with the police, you know. It will lighten his sentence."

I didn't know. So, that's why they let Alex go, to help them catch the others. Cool! They were caught now. All of them. It was over. It made me feel good, satisfied, but weird, though. What would I do now?

Why, I would play in the Jungle with the Girls. We could play our innocent games. All our mysteries would be pretend, from now on. The bad guys would be pretend. We would be children and snuggle with our mommies and daddies and be safe. That is what I wanted. I said good-bye to the officer and rode home. There was no one to run me off the road except the tourists gawking at the water views and not paying attention.

I made a detour, though. I had to talk to Billy. No matter how tired I was, something was still bothering me. I guess I had been trying to ignore it, but it wouldn't go away. I kept telling myself that it didn't matter. Maybe it didn't . . .

When I got to the Nor'easter, I went down the alley to the parking lot and peered in the back door.

"Pssst! Billy!" He looked up from his work and came out.

"What's up?" he asked.

"A lot, but I can't tell you everything right now. The police caught Smythe's friend, Mr. Greasy. That creep actually shot a gun at us! At Lowndes River!"

"No!" Billy couldn't believe it.

"Yes! But what I need to know is the relationship between the harbor master and this bunch. I know she's involved, but I don't know how. She and Knowles are both from Wallington, but I'm not sure if there's a connection there or if it's just a coincidence."

"My brother doesn't want to answer any more questions."

"Oh please! Just this once?" I sounded like a baby, but this usually worked on my parents, even though it annoyed them. And it probably annoyed Billy.

Billy looked tired. Working two jobs was a lot. He constantly went from the yacht club to the restaurant and back again. I wished that he could get a reward for all the help he had given us, but there was no one to give a reward. I guess the satisfaction of knowing that we did the right thing had to be enough.

"I'll see what I can do. We might as well investigate all facets of the mystery, if we can. Leave no lea unturned," he was saying, as his boss bellowed "BILLY! STOP THAT YAKKING AND GET BACK TO WORK!"

# Chapter Twenty-Three

turned and rode my bike out of the parking lot, down Main Street, and to the police station. I couldn't stop now. I might as well find out the latest news on Mr. Greasy. Fortunately the chief was in his office and asked me in, even though Officer Personality said that he was too busy and couldn't see me.

"You alright?" he asked, showing real concern in his eyes, which were wrinkled and slanted like John Wayne's (you know, that cowboy in the old movies). That character who shot at you won't say a word! We don't know who he is, except that he's a friend of Smythe's, and he tried to run you over with a motorboat. You girls seem to attract trouble like a magnet!"

"We don't try," I complained. "We were just in the wrong places at the wrong times, that's all."

"But you started asking questions and because of that we now have that creep in custody and the Coast Guard is bringing the rest of them in now. The whole gang and their suppliers. The suppliers tried to start a shootout but thought better of it. We've got them all now, thanks to Alex Nickerson and you girls," he said. "I think you girls should get the reward. No one listened much to any of you. Nickerson said that you got him to turn himself in . . ."

"He said that?" I asked, incredulous.

"Yep. His reward is that he won't go to jail for as long as the others. Of course Smythe will get longer for the murder," added the chief.

"Is there really a reward?" I asked, thinking of Billy.

"Yep. There are some civic organizations that want to see an end of this drug business. Of course we do, too. It's ruining some of our youth here."

A reward sounded good. Then I asked, "By the way, did the harbor master ever let you know whose boat that man was using when he shot at us?"

"She didn't call us, so we called her. It turns out the boat belongs to Larry Knowles, one of the Smythe crew. It seems it's the same one he used to run you kids over."

That did it! She was involved and wanted to protect Knowles for some reason. Should I tell the chief? Would he do anything about it? I decided to wait for Billy to do my detective work for me if he could. I thanked the chief and rode home.

# Chapter Twenty-Four

After dinner a truck pulled into the driveway. It was Billy.

"Hey," he called to me as I went to meet him in the yard. "You left your sunblock at the club!"

"Oh! Thanks!" I exclaimed. It wasn't my sunblock, but I knew that it was just an excuse.

In a low voice he said, "Knowles is Jan's cousin! It seems that she was kind of wild in her younger days and she doesn't want people here to know about it. Somehow Smythe found out, and she's afraid to anger him for fear he'll tell and she'll lose her job and be run out of town! Knowles probably blabbed it when he was drunk. She's afraid Knowles might talk too."

"Wow!" I exclaimed. "That explains everything, almost. That's great, Billy. Thanks for the information. But why is Knowles digging clams if he makes so much money fishing and selling drugs? That doesn't make sense."

"My brother says that he's always bellyaching about his ex-wife and his kids going to college. I guess he's just trying to be a good ex-husband and father!"

"Yeah, right! A great role model. Dealing drugs and selling rotten shellfish. Ruining people's lives and stomachs so his kids can do better in life than he did Really makes sense!" I said in disgust.

"Well, it makes sense to him," said Billy. "Lots o people justify doing wrong when it makes the lives of thei families a little easier. His family probably has no idea, o they don't care."

The world was a strange place. I decided to take th Girls with me on Wednesday to have a little talk with th harbor master. Why didn't I just tell the police? Becaus I thought she might be more honest with us. Why Because we were just kids. It was Plan C.

# Chapter Twenty-Five

First, the Coast Guard called early the next morning to let me know that the whole Smythe gang and their drug suppliers were in the county jail a few towns away. Since all of them had been caught "in the act," they would all get sent to prison for a long time. That was good news.

Then the police chief called. He related the same news, but there was one problem, he said. "Smythe was buying supplies with his crew on the Tuesday morning the murder occurred. They were all together, except Knowles. He says he was sleeping, but of course he has no witnesses."

"So *he's* the one!" I shouted.

"We're not sure. Since there's no body and no probable cause . . ." the chief was saying.

"He must have had a cause. Can't you investigate? You have to find something!" I almost screamed. He had to go, he said, and hung up the phone.

No, no, no. A thousand times NO!!! This couldn't be. I wanted this case to be over. I wanted my life back. I had had enough mystery. There was only one person left to question. I called the Girls and set up an emergency meeting at Laura's house.

# Chapter Twenty-Six

"You're crazy," said Mollie, when I told them Plan C had to be activated. "She won't tell us anything. You'll just make it worse. Then she'll have time to make up some story to tell the police, and she'll never get caught for her involvement, whatever it is. Maybe she's selling drugs too. That could be her deep, dark secret. She might even attack us. You don't know!"

We sat on lawn chairs in Laura's backyard, high above the harbor. Her house was between the club and Mollie's house. It was an old house, very quaint, but the kitchen and bathrooms were brand-new. Old kitchens and bathrooms are creepy. I know because that's what we have at our cottage.

It was another great day, but I couldn't enjoy it. I was impatient to solve the mystery. I wanted to be free. Plus I just wanted to finish the job. Why were these girls always fighting me now? Maybe I would have to forget about them and go to Billy again, but I didn't want that. We had brought in Mr. Greasy. All the rest of the gang was behind bars. We had accomplished so much together. Why were they doing this now?

"Come on Girls! She's the only one left that we know of. She might have some good information."

"Look! There she is now!" exclaimed Laura. Sure enough, Jan was in the harbor snooping around, looking for illegal moorings. Laura's father had told us that people drop a concrete block with a rope and float tied to it to use it as a mooring, but one is supposed to get permission from the town first. The problem was the town wasn't giving out permission because the harbor was already overcrowded with all the legal moorings!

"O.K." said Abigail. "Let's go."

We trotted down a narrow sandy path, between towering wild rose bushes, to the shore. The roses' scent was thick and sweet, but we had no time to enjoy it. The tide was so low that we could wade out to Jan.

"Hi there!" Mollie called. "May we talk to you?"

"Sure," she replied with a decidedly sinister look on her face. "Hop in," she offered. We hopped into her boat. "Sit down," she said, pointing to the bottom of the boat. As we sat she accelerated a little and moved her boat out toward the channel. We looked at each other nervously. Why were we obeying her?

"What's up, girls?" she asked with a sneer. I didn't have a good feeling about this.

"We just wanted to ask you a few questions about

the *California Girl* case," said Laura. She had suddenl
become courageous!

"Well, what is it you want to know?" she asked
We couldn't see well from where we sat, but it seemec
that she was headed out of the harbor into the sound
This wasn't good.

"We want to know why you're protecting Knowle
to the extent that you aren't doing your job properly,"
Mollie blurted out.

Jan laughed. She looked really scary!

"I might as well tell you. It doesn't matter now
He's my cousin. He used to party with me, and we dic
drugs together when we were younger. I stopped rea
quick after getting caught and doing jail time, but tha
drunk had to tell Smythe. Now I can't do anything, or
they'll tell and then I'll lose my job." As she looked intc
her past, her eyes weren't seeing where we were going,
which was out to sea!

"Then I was checking moorings last week when I
saw that drifter on Smythe's boat. He called me over and
told me that he suspected Smythe of being involved with
drugs. I tried to tell him that he was mistaken, but he
wouldn't quit. He said he'd tell the police, if I wouldn't
listen to him. I got on board and tried to talk some sense
into him. He tried to grab me. I stepped back, and he

lipped on the wet deck. He fell back against the corner of he fish bin. It went right through his skull . . ."

Wow. Her description brought back memories. I wanted to cry, throw up, faint. She was the murderer. We'd never suspected her. It had been an accident, just s she had suggested, but she had concealed it. She couldn't tell, but it would have been better for her if he had, because now it was too late. Maybe it was too late for us too.

"What did you do with the body?" I asked.

She laughed again. She had lost her mind!

"I took it out to sea. Weighted it down real good. t's gone now. Fish food." She laughed some more. "Just ike you," she added, looking down at us.

I jumped up and looked around. We were passing a boat working the fish traps in the middle of the sound.

"Help! Help!" I shrieked. The other Girls stood up also and began to scream and wave their arms. It was Mollie's neighbor, Howard, and his crew. They looked up and stopped their work, puzzled. But they left the trap and moved toward us.

The harbor master's boat was now speeding out o sea at a much faster rate than Howard's old dory. Jan suddenly left the helm and rushed back to us and heaved us overboard one by one. We didn't resist.

She sped into the distance.

Howard came along and hauled us out of the briny deep, you know, the water. It was a good thing we all know how to swim and to stay afloat by treading water. We were shaken, for sure. We breathlessly huddled together as Howard covered us up with his bright yellow foul weather gear.

"What happened?" he asked. He couldn't imagine why we had been on the harbor master's boat and why she had thrown us overboard.

We explained the whole story from beginning to end. Of course he had heard of the drug bust and he knew that something was going on with the harbor master, but he had kept out of it. Now, seeing she had intended to kill us, he wasn't so sure that he had done the right thing.

"Sorry, girls. I shoulda helped ya, but what if I had been wrong? It would have made my life miserable!" What a big baby he was!

"We could have followed your leads without anyone knowing where we got our information," Mollie declared. "We always protect our sources." She was talking like a pro! Maybe next time Howard would be a more responsible citizen!

Howard radioed the Coast Guard, and they

ent the cutter after Jan.

We were taken to shore and met by the police and Coast Guard. After answering many questions, our parents, who had been contacted, came to get us. They were surprised that we had gotten into trouble again but comforted us. We were all glad that it was finally over. Really over.

I was sure that our parents had been talking among themselves about our mystery. I hoped that they were proud of us. I was proud of us.

On our way home I asked Mom and Dad about Jan. "Can someone do drugs and then stop and become normal?" I asked. I was wondering if she could have been a decent person and have done a good job if her past hadn't been haunting her.

"Of course, dear," said Mom. "Lot's of people tried drugs, back when we were in high school and college, but they stopped and went on with their lives. They discovered that drugs didn't give them what was promised."

"What do drugs promise?" I was curious.

"They promise happiness, good feelings, insight. But one finds out that one is hurting one's body, confusing one's mind, and one ends up feeling deceived," continued Mom.

"How do you know, Mom? You never tried drugs, did you?" She gave Dad a nervous side glance. was devastated!

"Mom! Dad! How could you? You're my parents How could you be drug addicts? You're no better than that gang of drug dealers who just got put in jail" I was hysterical. All the excitement of the day, heaped on top of the last week of trauma, was too much for me with this revelation added to it.

"We are not and were not drug addicts," corrected Dad. "We were foolish and tried drugs that we thought would help us to be better people. We thought it was harmless and fun. We had read and heard that it would open our eyes to our inner selves and to the supernatural world. Now that I think of it, it was similar to what the Devil told Adam and Eve in the Garden of Eden! It was an empty promise of forbidden knowledge. We were deceived and could have died, literally. We were wrong and never tried it again."

"I can never forgive you," I sobbed. We were home now. Mom tried to hug me, but I pulled away from her and ran to my little room, slamming the door and throwing myself onto my bed, even though I was still wet and soggy. How could my parents do this to me? Especially now, after all I had gone through?

After a while the phone rang. I answered on the extension in my room. It was the Coast Guard. They couldn't find Jan and had notified the other authorities to keep a lookout for her, but they were giving up for now. I felt sorry for Jan. Had she jumped overboard? Did she swim to shore, to go off to start a new life? Whatever she did, I thought she should have told the truth. Maybe if she were caught now she would have to serve time in jail for hiding the body and trying to kill us, but she still had hope.

Before all this had happened, if the townspeople had found out about her past, I was sure that they would have forgiven her, if she had really changed. People are generally forgiving, but Jan hadn't even tried to find out.

But wait a minute! What about my Mom and Dad? Why couldn't I forgive them? They were my parents, that's why. They were supposed to be perfect. How could I look up to them, if they had broken the law and done something so terrible in the past? I couldn't forgive them! Or could I?

I slowly walked into the kitchen where my parents were eating blackberries and cream. Mom and Dad looked up at me. I hugged them both and started crying again.

"We're sorry to disappoint you, dear," Mom said.

"But your Dad and I thought that it would be better to te
you the truth. To let you know that we made a foolis
mistake and hopefully to prevent you from doing th
same thing, with worse results."

"You were right. I forgive you. I'll get over it. Tha
was the Coast Guard on the phone. They can't find Jar
I was thinking that if maybe she had been honest, sh
could have been forgiven and could have done a good jo
as harbor master."

"She wasn't doing a good job, in my opinion," sai
Dad. "But neither are the selectmen!"

"That's another issue," interrupted Mom as sh
fixed a bowl of berries for me. "It's possible that if sh
had confessed, she would have been free to do a bette
job, but we'll never know. She may have lost her job."

As we finished our snack, the phone rang again
The police chief told us that the civic organizations wer
going to give us a reward. I thought that Billy should ge
it. Without him, we would never have solved the mystery
But Billy got all his information from his brother.
thanked the chief and decided to talk to the girls and Bill
at the club the next day, Thursday.

# Chapter Twenty-Seven

normal summer day on the Cape. Foggy. Uncertain if
e could sail, we sat on the gray, weathered wooden
enches. I applied my sunblock because I knew that
armful sun rays can get through fog. The Girls and I
hispered about Jan and the reward. Something sad and
omething happy. Yes. Billy's brother should get the
eward, we decided. We planned to tell Billy after class.

Class began. We were going to learn how to use a
ompass. It was a fun class. Some of the kids had heard
rom their parents about our mishap the day before.
hey had heard that someone had shot at us, but they
idn't know that it was connected to the sinking of the
*Minnow*. They didn't know yet that we'd solved the murder
nystery, but they had heard that we'd helped with the
rug bust, a big item in the local, as well as state, news.

Apparently the drugs were coming up from the
outh, the suppliers making stops along the seaboard. We
vere celebrities now, but we didn't encourage our class-
nates. We wanted it to be a private experience for the Eel
Grass Girls (and Boy).

After class we took Billy aside and asked him what

he thought about giving the reward to his brother. H
thought it would be a great idea.

"He's acting awfully strange, though," he said. "H
seems really upset that Jan is gone. I asked him about i
He said that he kind of had a crush on her."

"What? On her?" We couldn't believe it.

"Yeah, but he knew it would never work. Since h
cared about her, he was reluctant to give us information.

"But he did and he helped us. Will he accept th
reward?" Laura asked.

"I'll talk to him," he said. "Got to go. I have a
instructors' meeting now."

After lunch at Laura's (her mom had planned
celebration lunch to honor us for our great detectiv
work), we lounged around and went for a swim, i
spite of the fog. On my way home I stopped by th
Nor'easter. Billy was at work and told me that he ha
spoken to his brother.

"He suggested that the money should go to the Fis
Fry. That's a local club that organizes activities to kee
kids off drugs. By the way, he decided to stop drinkin
and hanging out with bums. He's going to spend his tim
working with the kids at the 'Fry'. He said drinking is
problem here too. He's the perfect person to speak ou
against it!" I couldn't agree more!

As I rode home I felt happy. The fog made me feel damp all over and a little cool. My wet bathing suit had soaked through my clothes. I loved this kind of day, though. On Friday the Girls and I planned to meet at the Eel Grass Palace to play and then have lunch at the Clam Bar on the river.

# Chapter Twenty-Eight

"Can you believe we were almost killed as we sat in th[is] very place only three days ago?" asked Abigail.

You Girls are the best!" I exclaimed. "We stu[ck] together. You all risked your lives to solve this myster[y.] We *did the right thing*. We are the invincible Eel Grass Girls[!]" I shouted out. We all yelled and whistled. The touris[ts] fishing off the bridge stared at us.

"It was pretty scary," admitted Laura. "A lot of it. [I] can't believe that we really did all those things! Had ou[r] boat sunk. Rowed out to the *California Girl* at nigh[t.] Followed the truck full of drugs. Got shot at. Searche[d] for Mr. Greasy when he had a gun."

"Got thrown overboard!" continued Mollie. "Wo[w!] Wait 'til I tell my friends at school! What a summer!"

"Our friends won't believe us. Only Laura will [be] the real hero. Everybody in this town knows all about [it.] They know that it's all true," I said. "It's enough myste[ry] to last a life time. I'm looking forward to a nice norm[al] rest of the summer."

"Not to change the subject," said Mollie very slow[ly.] We all looked at her. I didn't like the I-kno[w]

omething-you-don't-know tone of her voice. "My
riend Louie showed me an old house on Snow Pond
esterday on the way to Abigail's." She paused and took
deep breath. "I think it's haunted."

"Oh, come on!" protested Laura. "There's no
uch thing!"

"Wait 'til you hear what happened," she continued.
ut, that's another story...

Rachel Nickerson Luna learned to sail at Sea Pin
Camp, Brewster, Cape Cod, and Stage Harbor Yac
Club, Chatham, Cape Cod. She also crewed at the riv
Chatham Yacht Club. She won the 2000 Championsh
Award for the Stage Harbor Adult Sailing School.